PELICAN BAY SECURITY

LIFETIME
Risk

USA TODAY BESTSELLING AUTHOR

MEGAN MATTHEWS

Edited by Amanda Brown

PROLOGUE

The oversized black beast roars, charging directly at my body. I stumble and waste a precious second staring at the small butterfly caught between its teeth as the beast runs into my side headfirst, knocking me to the ground. The pavement eats away at my skin and I slide a short distance, but I don't notice the pain in my leg until one of the other forest animals yells.

"Oh my God, look at her leg!"

More words are volleyed in the area surrounding where my body lays on the ground, but it's difficult making out what they say. A persistent wail fills the area, but not one like I expect. This isn't the ambulance coming to my rescue. No. It's worse. My head shakes back and forth, and with an unsteady hand, I reach out to silence the alarm on my phone. The ever present 7 a.m. warning it's time to start the day's madness.

Madness is the only way to describe a morning when you're the mother to a two-year-old.

The sound does more than wake me. It also wakes Emma, and I catch her cries from the other room. Without a second thought, I move my legs from the bed and grab the left one as pain rockets through my body. I flop back on the pillow and suck in large deep breath, doing my best to work through the shooting needles sensation in my ankle.

"There, there, little Emma, I've got you," a man's voice filters down the hallway in between flashes of pain.

I tense, making the leap from pain to terror, but not able to move. It doesn't last long as realization of the moment comes fast. No one is trying to kidnap my child, but the reality might be almost as bad.

There's a big bulky, hunky, former Navy SEAL in my apartment.

The same one who hit me with his truck and severely twisted my favorite ankle bone. *Yes, it's perfectly normal to have a favorite bone.* Earlier, the truck driver of doom promised to take care of us until someone from my family could arrive, but I secretly hoped he'd been kidding. I didn't need the man who almost killed me trying to nurse me back to health. What kind of sicko would that make me?

There are not enough pain pills in existence for me to survive having Nate Bellamy in my space.

1

I've used crutches one time in my life. Halfway through seventh grade field day I twisted my other ankle on the long jump. Back then I sucked at using the long pieces of wood to make my way through the school halls, and my skills hadn't improved with the years. Tired after only a few feet of hobbling my way down the apartment hallway, I lean against the wall pretending to inspect the paint job rather than resting my flabby arms. Emma laughs and darts between her doorway and the hallway, her long blonde hair a wild mess flowing behind her head.

"You're up," Nate says, as I pass into the open area of the living room. He's awake and much too bright-eyed for this early in the morning. Plus, when did he get here and who let him in my apartment?

These important questions will need to wait. I give the super-hot guy a silent nod and concentrate on using the crutches to take my stiff leg to the couch without falling on my ass and doing more damage.

He scrambles behind and pulls a pillow from the side, placing it on the coffee table and helping to adjust my ankle and protective boot on top. It's so nice... and annoying. He hit me with his truck. He doesn't get to be kind to me now. I'd be pissy to him, but the truth of the matter is I need all the help I can get.

"You want to make sure and keep your foot propped. Did you take a pain pill?" he asks, each question coming quicker than the last and leaving no time for me to answer any of them.

I let the full weight of my leg fall on the pillow and only wince twice with its progress. I can't see it because the compression boot hides the affected area, but underneath the black plastic, the bottom of my leg is swollen with a blackish purple bruise marring my pale skin. "No, I haven't yet."

His face falls, his brown eyes losing luster as they narrow in my direction with accusations etched in their depths. "You want to stay ahead of the pain, Josie."

"Yes, I know." I nod. No one wants to walk around in pain—least of all a wimp like me. "But I want to make sure I'm alert to take care of Emma today."

His forehead pinches together in question. "I'm here to take care of Emma. You're supposed to relax."

Emma darts into the hallway quietly and I'm already aware of where she's going. To flush something down the toilet. "Where is Emma?" He's been here less than a day and he's let his guard down already. He won't make it an afternoon in my apartment before he passes me off to another victim.

Nate blinks, and his eyes search the living room, but Emma's not here. He smirks and shrugs a shoulder, but worry and fear grow in his expression. I recognize the expression because I so often wear it myself.

"She's just waiting for breakfast. I'll get her," he lies.

"Uh-huh."

Nate turns on a heel, a toilet flushes further down the hall, and I wince, hoping it was nothing important lost down the drain this time. Since she became obsessed with the toilet about two months ago, I've done my best to lock valuables up or keep them on high shelves, but somehow she always finds something to flush. Thankfully it's a large building with the pipes to match. Usually.

Nate's gone longer than I would like and worry builds in my stomach. I still haven't figured out who let him in my apartment. With slow but sure movements I inch my way off the couch. I've never been great at sitting still for long periods. Halfway to the hallway a loud pop and plume of smoke whips out from the small galley kitchen in the apartment.

"Nate?" I call, trying not to panic even as I move my crutches quicker, risking certain death when I fall on my face. I'm only five-foot-five but my nose would not appreciate being squished. "What's going on in the kitchen?"

"Don't worry. I making everyone breakfast," he yells, somewhere down the hallway, and whatever he says afterward is covered by Emma's laughter. He's cooking something and chasing my child through the apartment? Those two things do not mesh.

He said not to worry, but I can't help my growing concern. The ends of my crutches catch on the carpet when I don't lift them up high enough, but I manage to make it to the kitchen without falling on my face.

My eyes water with the haze billowing out of the

small area. I twist the knob, turning the stove off, but a steady stream of smoke continues to rise from a blackened pan with what looks like burned and shriveled eggs. The smoke tenderloins reach up toward the ceiling as if calling for help from whatever torture he's put them through this morning. A stack of dishes rises over the edge of the sink and there're bits of scrambled egg squashed to the floor. I'm not sure who made breakfast—Nate or Emma.

How did all this damage happen in the few minutes it took me to turtle walk from my bedroom to the living room? How long has he been here?

The one lesson I learned since becoming a parent is that it's easier to stay in front of the mess than to come up behind it. If you're continuously cleaning, you're not trying to catch up at the end of the day. With one crutch leveled against the counter, I survey the rest of the space while turning on the water in the sink.

Dried food is stuck on most of the dishes along with other unrecognizable bits that won't make it through my cheap dishwasher. The wash cycle reminds me of my husband's attempts in the bedroom. Whip the wand around three times, squirt liquid on everything, and then with a dying moan roll over and pass out.

With those results I'd rather do the dishes... and other things... by hand.

I mean, ex-husband.

There isn't much room, but as the sink fills with water I drizzle soap on top. It's possible the commercials are correct and it will help me get them clean before they go in the dishwasher.

After I get the dishes washed, my next task is getting

Nate out of my apartment. We met yesterday at the hospital, if you don't count the hour before when he hit me with his truck as a first impression, but I've learned very little about the former SEAL. He works for Ridge and helped my neighbor, Winnie when she had problems. That's it. My entire knowledge base of Nathan Bellamy can be summed up in less than a paragraph.

Maybe not everything.

His eyes are the deepest shade of brown. Light and dark are swirled together, so if you're not careful you could get lost in them for hours. But regardless of what *Cosmo* would say, having pretty eyes doesn't qualify him to be in my apartment taking care of me or Emma. The water bubbles close to the edge of the sink and I shut it off before grabbing the first pan to scrub. Nate's eyes aren't what worry me. It's his ability to create such a mess from a simple scrambled egg.

Dread builds as I scrub the pan. Who is this man? What if I let Winnie bring a serial killer into my life? He hit me with a truck after all. Was it not an accident? My divorce is final so Barry wouldn't get anything extra by killing me off at this point—besides custody of Emma.

"Have you ever been to jail?" I yell the question from the kitchen, holding the pan out like a weapon. My body stiffens and I'm ready to use the stainless-steel object like a bludgeon depending on his answer.

Nate peeks his head in the small kitchen opening, and I shove the pan under the water so he doesn't get suspicious. "No." His expression shows he's insulted by the question.

But you can't ever be too safe.

"Emma is in her high chair, but what do I do now?"

he asks as he eyes the large grey high chair placed at the round dining room table. Her hair wraps around her face, covering her eyes with the rest of it in her mouth.

Finished with the pan, I place it in the bottom rack of the dishwasher. "Now you give her eggs." Truthfully, she hasn't used the high chair in months but with me immobile, having her contained is a good idea.

"I don't need to feed her?" Nate asks.

"Nope, she'll just shove it right in her mouth." And everywhere else in the surrounding area. The floor, the table, the walls, but I leave those scary facts out. Best Nate sees for himself.

"Have *you* ever been to jail?" he asks while placing a plate of brown eggs in front of Emma.

Now the fun begins.

I tilt my head and roll my eyes. "Of course not." Although, after I walked in to find my husband screwing our babysitter on our bed in the middle of the day, I came very close. To my benefit, the responding officer didn't consider the Happy Meal box I chucked at their heads enough of a deadly weapon given the circumstances.

But I don't plan to tell Nate that story.

"What did you do in the military?"

The first piece of egg goes flailing as Nate and I watch its flight path before it crashes against the wall. Nate's face falls in shocked horror and he races to pick it off before dries. "I was a SEAL. It's special ops." He walks back into the kitchen with the slimy egg chunk cupped in his hand and his mouth open in disgust searching for a trash can.

"That's not an answer," I say, when he stops talking while wiping his hands over the under-sink trash.

"Most of my work is still classified, but we went where we were needed and helped other teams finish a mission in whatever way they needed. I've done recon and a little undercover work."

"Undercover work?"

Nate doesn't answer my question. Instead he stares at Emma's egg-covered face like she's a bomb set to explode. Little does he realize she's just warming up for the day. The eggs will only give her protein to keep her going. "Why is she eating her hair?"

"Because you didn't pull it back," I respond, turning back to my dishes. "There's a drawer of hair ties in the bathroom."

The room goes silent except for the happy sounds a feeding child makes as they destroy a parent's security deposit. When I finish rinsing off the last pan, there's a gasp and I turn fast ready to jump into mother mode. Gasps are never good.

2

There's no blood, but Emma has finished her eggs. Most of them found their way to the surrounding areas. "What did you do to her hair?" A large chunk of her hair–by no means all of it–is wrapped around a ponytail on the top of her head. The strands fall limply to one side and pieces stick out in every direction.

"I tied it up," Nate answers, his face proud.

That's going to be hell come bath time.

I grab the sponge and with one crutch finagle my way to the dining room table.

"What are you doing?"

The question catches me off guard. "Wiping down the table." Duh.

Nate steals the sponge from me and waves it around the tabletop, spreading eggs over the surface. "You're supposed to be resting. I'll take care of this."

Eggs fall to the floor and he steps in a clump, smooshing them into the carpet. Definitely not getting my security deposit back. After Barry cheated, I needed a fresh start away from everyone in my past life. I didn't just lose my husband to his affair. I also lost my best friend.

No, she wasn't the babysitter, but midway through the divorce, while she was comforting me with a carton of Ben and Jerry's, she slipped and let the truth out. She'd been aware of his ongoing dalliance for months and never told me. Her betrayal hurt almost as badly as Barry's. A best friend should always tell.

Nate finishes ruining my carpet and throws the sponge into the sink, landing the shot from a good eight feet away. I'm a little impressed. He can't drive, but with his height he might land a dunk.

Emma claps and pats at the high chair, but rather than get her out, I sit down in the chair next to her. Standing so long has tired me out and a slow ebb of pain has taken up resident in my leg—as if the bones themselves are pissed off I've taken such shitty care of them. Nate opens a laptop on his side of the table and taps away at the keys.

"Are you from Pelican Bay?"

He looks up to answer and then right back down again. "No, my aunt and uncle in Las Vegas raised me. They are the only family I have left."

"Do you go to see them often?"

I pepper him with the second question. "No, we don't see eye to eye."

"Oh, that's sad."

This time Nate fully lifts his head at my comment. "Not really. They make Harry Potter's guardians seem like loving parents."

"Oh." Well, that is a different situation then. His attention falls back to the screen, done with our conversation, but his answer only creates more questions. Did they lock him in a closet? A room under the stairs? When did Nate read Harry Potter? Did he find the ending was rushed or too drawn out? Would he agree they spent way too much time in the woods?

Nate types a few more seconds, but the ever-expanding list of questions continues to grow until I must ask. "Why did you leave the military?"

He winces and then lifts a shoulder in the air in a shrug. "Wasn't fun anymore."

"You left because it wasn't fun anymore?" Is the military supposed to be fun? "Why did you move to Pelican Bay?" It's like pulling teeth to get an answer out of the man. You'd think he'd be a little more giving since he almost killed me yesterday with his butterfly-eating truck.

Nate shrugs again but eventually lifts his attention and answers. "Ridge put together a new team of guys and asked for my help."

Ridge must be an important guy if he can ask and people move to a little town in Maine to work for him.

"Why did you move to Pelican Bay?" he parrots one of my questions back at me.

"Divorce and a fresh start. I took a job as an administrative assistant with the city in Clearwater."

"Where is your family?" Nate's as good of an interrogator as I am.

I'm much better at answering. "Bangor with my ex."

"You don't miss them?" he asks.

My attention falls, not sure how to answer his question, and I notice his laptop looks like mine. Although I guess most laptops are black. "Bangor isn't that far away. I still see them." Unfortunately.

I love my family, but my mother has a serious case of "I told you so" syndrome that I'm happy to be away from most days. She never liked Barry and hasn't wasted an opportunity to remind me of the fact now that we're not married.

"Are you planning to buy a house here?"

"Possibly?" That's a weird question. "Why?"

Nate spins the laptop around and on the screen are the images of a house I'd been looking at a few hours before the accident.

"Hey! That's my laptop." And my house. I hadn't gotten the chance to even set up a second showing yet and now with unknown medical bills, the house-buying prospect is fading away. But still, laptops are private. I'm not ready to share my dreams with Nate.

He pulls the computer back to his side of the table. "I didn't think you'd mind if I checked my email."

"But you didn't *just* check your email. You snooped through my stuff."

"It was open in the browser." He laughs, but I don't find it funny at all.

Emma cries, upset by my raised voice, and I stand up quickly to grab her without considering my hurt ankle. My knee hits the underside of the table and pain shoots up from my foot.

"Owww," I cry before sitting down hard.

Nate leaps from his chair coming to my side. His hands rest on my shoulders as I breathe trying to get the pain under control. "You need to be on the couch propping up your ankle."

"But Emma," I protest as he tries to help me stand.

"Let me take care of you. Then I'll get her." His voice is soft and full of wonderful promises, but he's clueless on what he's volunteering himself for when it comes to Emma.

BOREDOM KICKS itself into high gear about two hours later as I contemplate counting the number of speckles on my apartment's tiled ceiling. I'm not great at sitting still and doing nothing, which is what a serious sprain requires you to do. Thankfully, the doctors promised it at least wasn't a break. But a sprain is still a sprain, and until I'm able to get around better without searing pain shooting up my leg, I'm on desk duty.

Except desk duty is the couch in my living room with my foot propped up on a pillow over the coffee table. I hate being helpless. Yes, I agree with the doctors about being glad it wasn't broken. A twisted knee and sprained ankle are better than a break, but it's still a nuisance. He said a full two weeks off it, but by then the Disney Jr. theme song will cause me to lose my mind.

I also don't like the fact that practically a stranger — the same one who hit me with a truck — is watching my child play with blocks on the floor. He was the one to chase after her the last time the toilet flushed when neither of us were using the room, and most recently he ran off to figure out why it was so quiet in the hallway before he could drop off the laptop. At least if I had my laptop I could work.

I need the money, but I'm also concerned about my

job. The Environmental Quality Office in Clearwater is understaffed at the moment, and the more work I get done from my couch the better. I don't have enough hours at my part-time job to qualify for FMLA, and my inability to make it to the office for the next two weeks — until I get better at getting myself around — means I'm back to living off my savings account.

When I left Barry, I promised myself I'd never depend on someone else again, but that's what I am right now. At Barry's urging, I'd quit my job when I gave birth to Emma and believed all his lies about taking care of me for the rest of my life. It was such a wonderful idea—one I wanted so badly to be true.

There's a knock on the front door, the sound echoing from the living room of my apartment. The problem is, everything echoes in this apartment and half the time I get up to answer the door, it's someone knocking on a neighbor's door. Then I looked like the weirdo spying on everyone else in my hallway.

"Nate," I yell, hopeful it'll be him wasting his time going to check.

Hey, if he's here at my disposal I might as well use him. He hit me with his truck after all.

He doesn't answer. The last sound I heard from the hallway was the giggles of a two-year-old who figured out she's been caught doing something she shouldn't. Fear refused to let me ask what she'd done now.

The knock comes again and this time it's obviously from my apartment when the door rattles against the frame. With more effort than it should require, I find my crutches and plop my leg down from the pillow, making my way from the couch. It better be worth it. Like a huge ass box from Amazon with buckets of cash.

Except when I open the door, I'm met face-to-face with the last person I want to see. Now that I'm not madly in love with him, it's easy to see his flaws. Nose too big for his face, the balding spot on the back of his head, which I can't see from my angle but is there, and eyebrows that if he doesn't get ahold of them soon, he'll resemble a fuzzy caterpillar at a rave within the next five years.

"Barry." I try to greet him like you would greet anyone you've known for a lifetime but hate in the most abrasive way. However, I'm only able to pull off irritated. It's been a long day.

He takes a step into my apartment, his eyes on the boot covering my foot. "Josie, I heard the news, but wasn't sure it was true." His cologne, old man spice, fills the area around him. How did I once find it attractive? Nate has his own woods smell, like he sleeps with pine trees, and while I've never been a woods girl, I'd sniff him all day.

"What news is that?" My mind fills with lots of newsworthy bits he might have heard. How much I can't stand looking at him. How I hate he's breathing my air. Or that I've envisioned it was him being hit by a truck more times than is legal. I mean seriously, how is it he's the one who cheats, but I'm the one hit by a truck? Karma really is a bitch.

"Your Aunt Millie called and said you had an accident. Almost broke your ankle."

Oh, he's here about *that* news. Damn Aunt Millie. She was the one person on my side of the family who liked Barry. I always wondered if she'd flip and provide information for him. There was no other explanation for how he found out where Emma and I moved after first coming to Pelican Bay. I had to tell him eventually, only he showed up to inspect our new apartment and double check for safety the day we moved. I realized at that point I had a mole in the family.

"Yes, I hurt my ankle, but I'm not dead if that's what you hoped. You could have called rather than drive all the way here."

He sighs, rolling his eyes to the ceiling in a move that has pissed me off since we started dating. He's a teenager who was playing house with me but hasn't had the time to grow up yet. "Contrary to how you may feel about me, Josie, I don't wish you any ill will. I want what's best for our daughter."

"Yes, but the problem is Barry, you believe that is with you and not her mother where she belongs."

"I'm concerned about you and your health. If it's a bad sprain, you need to be resting. Do you have someone here to help you?"

If it is hurt? Did he just say that if it really is a bad sprain? Like I would fake a sprain. I don't get how you can be married to someone for so long and share a bed with them, yet know so little about that person.

How is it somebody who promised to love you for a lifetime gets wrapped up with the nanny and throws all your happiness away?

That's not quite true. Is it? Because his happiness wasn't thrown away. He just tossed mine in the garbage. In Barry's world he traded up for more happiness. I was last year's American Girl doll, the one who wears colonial American dress rags. And Lindsey is the newest version with a cute little sequin dress from the 1920s, happily living in the Jazz Era before the depression hits.

"How do you plan to take care of Emma?" he asks, crossing his arms over his chest.

"The same way I have every day since she was born."

Like having a sprained ankle makes me incapable of taking care of my child.

"It can't be easy and I'm sure the hospital gave you pain meds. I don't like you in this apartment alone with Emma while you're taking drugs." His words make me sound like I'm a drug addict getting hopped up in the bathroom.

My skin heats as anger builds, and even though I shouldn't, I picture Nate's big black truck running him down as I watch from the sidelines. *Oh no, Barry. Watch out.... Not.* I'd at least pretend to be upset.

For Emma's sake.

"I'm fine, as you can see."

Of course, just my luck, my balance takes a hit as I stand back up trying to let Barry see I'm fine taking care of myself. Thankfully I don't fall over on my ass and I'm able to regain my balance without my crutches. It requires me to take one small step back and I grimace through the pain.

"See?" Just from his smug face he thinks he's already won. "I'll take Emma off your hands until you're better. There's no way you can take care of her by yourself. Lindsey will be more suited."

My mouth falls open in shock. Was he always this rude and callous, or is it a new trait he picked up since our divorce?

"How dare you imply that I'm incapable of taking care

of our child? Is Lindsey still babysitting as her main source of income? Is that why you think she'd be so much better because she has experience? Which other daddies do you think she's having affairs with?"

Barry narrows his eyes in my direction. These are all insults we've used before, during, and after the divorce. "Lindsey is putting herself through school."

I'm sure she's is, except now her tuition payments come from what used to be my joint checking account.

"Well, how will she be able to take care of Emma if she's so busy studying human anatomy?" We all know whose anatomy she was studying not that long ago.

"Stop being ridiculous, Josie. The point remains the same. You cannot care for Emma alone in this apartment. You can either hand her over now with less trauma or I will get a judge involved."

Those words are enough to take my anger from pissed off to straight through the roof — the level of angry a woman can only express through tears and sometimes throwing things. How was I ever attracted to this man? I also drank cheap Boones Farm wine in my twenties. My standards were clearly much lower.

My fists clench and I inwardly swear at my eyes not to shed a tear. I refuse to let him see how he continues to hurt me. Because Barry is so sure of himself and his superiority, he would get a judge involved. And by the time it would take to drag it all out and get a court day, I'll be healed, but between the court costs and the stress it would all take its toll. And he knows it.

When it comes down to it, money always wins and the one thing Barry has a lot of is money.

"Josie, you didn't tell me it was Barry's day to pick

Emma up." Nate's booming voice carries from the hallway. It's not that he speaks rudely or harshly, but simply with authority. He so sure of every word he says.

I turn, just enough to not knock myself over on the crutches, and wipe away a tear while facing the other direction. He stands just at the start of the living room, Emma safely tucked between his arms. Her hair is lopsided and floppy, but she has a smile on her face and Nate ignores her attempts to bash his collarbone in with the oversized LEGO building block. For his part he doesn't seem fazed in the least even as his neck where she hits turns red.

"Who the fuck is that?" Barry asks.

I twist back to him. "Don't swear in front of Emma."

"I'm Nate," my brown-eyed savior says, stepping closer and attempting to put a hand around my shoulder. But the way I move my crutches makes for an awkward pose and he soon gives up on the embrace.

"And what are you doing in my wife's apartment?"

My eyes widen and my body goes stiff. "Ex-wife," I say with as much of venom as possible. He doesn't get to tote a wife and a girlfriend too. Not anymore.

If possible, Nate's smile widens, and he bounces Emma on his hip. "I'm here helping until Josie is back on her feet."

"That's very nice of you, I'm sure," Barry says. "I don't like it when people try to use my daughter to get in her mother's pants."

I gasp, not because he's so blunt, but because isn't that what he used our daughter for when he started screwing the nanny? Plus, Nate hasn't even seen my underpants.

Nate leans in a little closer, almost like he's about to

whisper something to Barry, but he ends up saying it loudly enough I have no problem hearing. "That's why I've got muscles, mate." He looks at the flabby skin on Barry's arms and dramatically cringes before Emma hits him again with the LEGO block.

I laugh and pinch my lips together before I'm caught. Barry is proud of himself and if you upset him too much, he'll make my life horrible.

"Emma has daycare for when you go to work. Right?" Barry asks. Funny how he remembers the daycare I use now when a few minutes ago I was incapable of taking care of Emma. As a new mother, I said I'd never put my child in daycare, so I hired a trained nanny to come to our home whenever I had an appointment or afternoon with my mother. Now I realize what a horrible decision that was, and I plopped Emma in the largest daycare center it in the county. She's had every sickness known to man, but I figure it's prepping her immune system for when she goes to school in a few years.

"Daycare? How can I let my girlfriend's child go to daycare when I'm capable of taking care of both of them? Plus, with Josie unable to work she'll be missing a paycheck, something I'm sure you, as a concerned father, care about and want to open up the checkbook and help with the extra expenses." Nate ends his short speech with a knowing smile and my heart blossoms for the man who a few hours ago I worried had a criminal record.

Barry and I both stand looking at him with our mouths open. Me because I can't believe he called me his girlfriend. He's doing it for shock value because that's something he should ask for approval on in advance.

"Well, um, things haven't been great at the firm, but I

can slip you extra grocery money. I can keep a record and make the courts take it out of future child support checks once you're back on your feet," Barry stumbles over himself getting all the words out.

This time it's my turn to roll my eyes. I may hate the trait, but I picked it up from him. "Don't worry about it. I hate to put you and Lindsey out. I have money saved."

His face reddens because we both know all the money came from with the generous divorce settlement my amazing lawyer was able to get me. I may have been sad about my divorce, but I wasn't stupid.

EMMA RESTS PEACEFULLY. Her little head with her hair rumpled across the pillow looks quiet and serene. When she sleeps, there's no evidence of the terror she possesses through her waking hours. She's like a little angel. I give her a quick kiss on the top of her head and then spend another minute trying to memorize this exact scene as I lean against the doorjamb.

When I turn into the hallway, my steps squash in the wet carpet. There's a clang and I hurry to close her door so the noise from the bathroom doesn't wake her.

Most of Nate's body blocks the view into the bathroom where he watches the maintenance man with his hands down the pipe. I hope the apartment complex pays their maintenance crew a lot. With a swish and squeak of rushing water, his hand comes up, his wrist wrapped in fake blonde doll hair.

"This looks to be the problem," he says staring in disgust at the doll. "You shouldn't try to flush things like this." He looks past Nate and makes eye contact with me, like I'm the one who flushed the head of a doll down the toilet. I don't plan to ask where the rest of her went.

Nate turns noticing my presence. "I'm sure it was an accident," he says, smiling as if he too wants to blame this on me.

The maintenance guy — whose name I still haven't learned — dumps the doll in the trash and I make a mental note to throw it away in the dumpster tonight. If Emma sees it, I'll never get it away from her until she flushes it again. The rest of the cleanup goes quickly as he reattaches the toilet and uses one of my nice brand-new bathroom towels to dry his hands of the toilet water.

A large fan at the end of the hallway spins on high, working to dry the carpets, but the evaporation is cold and before long I'm forced to leave the area so the cool air doesn't give me goosebumps.

The couch is a welcome haven when I truck my way to it and plop my foot back on the pillow, which has been stationed at the coffee table all day. It's barely 8 o'clock, but it feels as if today I've lived a lifetime. They say the days are long, but the years are short. It's a bunch of bullshit if you ask me. The days are long and a few of them longer than others, aging us enough for an entire year. Barry and I planned for four children before things went to crap right after having Emma. I planned to get pregnant right after her first birthday, but our happy marriage never made it that far. Looking at the current state of my home, it may have been a blessing.

What if Barry is right and I can't take care of Emma as well as he could? It's the pain from my ankle and the exhaustion from the day talking, but he has a point. My shit isn't together when I'm 100 percent healthy. I wouldn't have been hurt if she hadn't gotten out of my grasp and run in the middle of the parking lot. What mother lets her child almost get hit by a truck?

"You should be fixed now. Just try not flush any non-organic material down the pipes," the lumbering maintenance man comments and then walks through my living room, his wet boots leaving prints across the dry carpet. What's a little more water, I suppose?

I wave his direction in a silent thank you and Nate walks him to the door, discussing wax rings and side bolts. I'm too tired to fake interest.

The couch fluffs up when Nate sits down at the other end. His movements jostle my leg and I grit my teeth trying hard not to cry out.

"Sorry."

I breathe deep. "It's fine."

It's one of those situations where if one part of my feeble attempt at building a wall of strength breaks, the whole thing will come down around me. I've held it together this long today, and I just need to get to bed so I can try again tomorrow.

"Do you want to watch TV?" Nate asks.

My head turns slowly in his direction contemplating what answer he expects me to give. "No, I want you to go home."

The words are meaner than I intend them to sound, but I'm tired and I need a few minutes alone.

Nate shakes his head. "Come on now, Josie. We've had a long day. Let's watch TV and relax."

My teeth gnash together. I'm so tired of men not listening to me. "No, Nate, I want you to leave."

3

"You don't want me here?" he asks, as if the sheer idea I would want to spend time without him hovering over me is unimaginable.

I shake my head so he can see. "I want to be alone and go to bed."

His face hardens and his lips pinch together in agitation. I don't get what he's upset about. I'm the one with an ex-husband trying to steal her daughter and an overflowing toilet. He gets to leave here tonight acting like he did a good thing helping me out today and enjoy his nice normal life leaving me and this mess as a distant memory.

"Fine," he says the word breathily. "Be that way, Josie. I'm here trying to help, but I'm done. You've made it known you don't want me around, so fine. Stay here by yourself."

He stands from the couch, the back of his polo shirt coming untucked from his jeans, and without a second glance back he storms out of my apartment and life as fast as he barreled into it.

I don't watch him leave, preferring to be alone with my sadness, but the heavy sound of the door rattles me a little too much. It's enough to cause a small crack that topples the wall I worried about moments earlier. If I was more dramatic, I'd lie on the couch and have a meltdown in all my glory, but my ankle hurts too much to move it so I'm left to cry into my own two hands in the quiet of the living room.

In my younger years I never imagined how pathetic I'd be at this age. I thought I'd have my shit together at this point. Great big tears roll down my face as bitterness steals more of my day. I'm not sure where I went wrong in life. I had so many plans. So many things I would accomplish by this age. But instead of my happy little family of growing children who I would dress to look alike for family pictures and take on weekend picnics, I'm here alone with soggy hallway carpeting and a child, while precious, I can't wait until her first day of school. More than once over the last few months I considered starting a countdown to the very happy day. I'm sure good mothers don't experience these kinds of thoughts. A good mother would relish every moment she has with her child and definitely wouldn't let her flush shit down the toilet while she argues with her own mother on the phone in the living room.

I'm right in the middle of a good misery cry, one of those kinds where once you finish crying your body will be lighter and less chaotic, when the front door opens and slams shut again.

I should probably be concerned about robbers, but I don't possess more energy in me tonight. If someone is here to take my second-hand furniture, then so be it.

"No!" At first I think Nate's outspoken word is in response to me being robbed, but then I remember he stormed out a few moments ago and all the robbery comments were in my head.

I do my best to glance at him by the door without turning my body and causing more pain.

"What the hell, Josie?" Nate questions, sprinting to my side by the couch. "Did you hurt yourself?"

He presses his hand on my boot, moving the crutches out of his way. "No. Can't you just leave me here to cry in peace?" In my mind the words are hard and full of strength, but in reality, they come out choked between each sob like a sad woman who wants to break in the privacy of her own home without an audience. Is that so much to ask?

Nate rests on his knees at the base of the couch looking at me with sad eyes. "Oh, Josie."

His pity makes me cry harder. I've never been a cute crier, which is why I prefer not to do it in front of people. I don't have a mirror, but I don't need one to know my face is red and my nose swells so I resemble Rudolph having an allergy attack.

Even though I want nothing more than for him to turn around a walk out of the apartment acting like he never saw me break down, Nate does the exact opposite. Which I've found he normally does. He slides up on the couch beside me and one of his big thick arms wraps around my shoulders pulling me close and allowing me to cry my tears into his armpit. It's a good smelling armpit. A soft pine tree.

"Tell me what's wrong," he pries.

I shake my head no but then began talking. "Is so hard, Nate. I've been strong for so long but I don't think I can do it anymore." My second sentence gets choked off by a sob but there's so much more I want to say. How can I raise Emma if I'm emotionally unstable?

"You don't need to do it alone anymore, Josie. You have help. I will be here to take care of you until you are one hundred percent better."

And then what will I do? I live in a town where I know no one. There's no help and even though I haven't admitted it to myself, my job barely pays the bills. Between working, taking care of Emma, and trying to sleep at least six hours a night, my life is ridiculous. Is this the way it will be until she turns eighteen? I'll never make it.

When the tears slow, I pull back from his embrace. "I'm sorry. It's just that I suck so much."

"You don't suck," he says, managing a smile.

I nod my head. "Nate, I don't know what happened." Years ago — what feels like forever but wasn't too far away — I had been cool. Popular in high school even. I had moves and a fashionable wardrobe, but those days are gone now.

"I hit you with my truck. If it's anyone fault, it's mine." The carefree smile he sported moments ago falls. "There's no way I can say sorry enough or do enough to make you feel better. The least I can do is stay here and take care of you and try my best to make it right."

I slap his shoulder. "Things went wrong a lot further back than when you hit me."

Like way back in high school, the day I met Barry. Yet, as soon as I visualize it, I force away the thought. Without that jackass in my life, I would've never given birth, and life wouldn't be worth it without her here. Even if she does tempt me to insanity every day.

"Well, I'm going to do my best to make sure life is perfect from here on out," he says, squeezing me tightly. "I promise."

I laugh, a small desperate chuckle. "Then you need a lot of Oreos." Oreos are god's gift to America. Cheap, but full of delicious flavor. There are even special holiday editions. An Oreo can fix a bad day whether relished in front of the TV or shoved in your mouth in the kitchen during the few seconds your child isn't looking. Oreos can make any problem better... except this one.

THE BEDROOM curtain is pulled back and I'm washed with heavy morning sunlight. Not the good kind that wakes you up from a peaceful slumber with ease so you can greet the day with a smile. No, it's the bad kind. The kind that rips you from a happy dream and tells you to get the hell out of bed and face another day of your life.

It's possible I may not be over my slight depressive mood from yesterday.

"Rise and shine." Nate's voice is way too cheery for this early in the morning. He's obviously guzzling coffee before he gets here, or worse, he's a morning person.

With the covers pulled over my head, I try to pretend

I'm still sleeping, but with a single hand he pulls them down exposing my face to the sun. On my lap he places a tiny tray that Emma uses for her tea parties. On top of the blue flower-pattern tray is a plate with eggs and two pieces of bacon, a fork, and a paper napkin. At the bedside table Nate places a tall glass of orange juice.

He fluffs the end of the bed covers and smiles at me like he's proud of what he's accomplished. Frankly it all reminds me of a scene from *Cinderella*, but that could be because it's Emma's current favorite movie, which means we watch it at least three times a day. I've got *Cinderella* on the brain.

"Thank you," I spit out before Nate leaves me alone in the bedroom with more food than I've had for breakfast in the last two years. The scene is different from the one yesterday.

He smiles back at me. "Take your time eating. I have everything under control."

Yesterday, I saw what he considered under control, but I haven't eaten breakfast, let alone breakfast alone, in months.

I wash down my morning pain pill with the glass of orange juice and eat the eggs in under five bites before I remind myself to calm down and chew slower. There are no devious little giggles coming from the living room and besides a steady clatter of pots and pans, nothing sounds as if it's breaking.

It's a pleasant morning.

A different scene than the one I went to bed with last night. After I let out two years of tears and relayed my entire life history and the ugly divorce while Nate cradled me on the couch, he put me to bed. Tucked me in and everything. Before he left, he said he'd see me in the morning, but I thought I'd scared him away for good. I was only 25 percent certain it wasn't all a dream.

Once the eggs are finished, he hasn't come back to collect the tray. There's no way I can carry it while using my crutches, so I abandon the dirty dishes to the bed top. With more grace than I had with the crutches yesterday I meander my way out to the hallway.

The carpet still squishes and squashes when my crutches make contact, the large fan the maintenance workers set up yesterday blowing a steady stream of air down the walkway. Hopefully the carpet will be dry soon so we can stop living in a wind tunnel.

I brace for impact when I hit the living room, my eyes squeezed so tightly I only open one at a time. When they're both open and surveying the space, panic builds and a small wall closes in around my heart with every breath. The living room is way too clean. What if last night was a dream and now I've woken up in the twilight zone? I died and rather than heaven I've gone to hell where Emma will be two forever.

There are no toys on the floor or eggs on the ceiling. My daughter who runs around room like an early morning tornado sits on the couch. Her eyes are engrossed in the morning episode of her favorite Disney Jr. show. I try not to let her watch too much TV, but if I had known peace like this existed, I'd have turned it on more often. She's even dressed, which sometimes doesn't happen until after she gets to daycare. Don't judge me. I'm not the only mom who's dressing a screaming child in the lobby at 7:30 a.m. Her hair is even done. Well, done enough for me. He's gone with pigtails today although the right side one is placed at least four inches lower than the left side. It makes it seem as if she is tilting her head in question. But it's not in her mouth, so a win for Nate.

"Nate?" I call into the otherwise empty room.

He pops his head out from the kitchen, a soapy pan in his hands. "Yup."

"Is everything okay?" Have the lot of them been abducted by aliens?

With caution, he takes a full step out of the kitchen and I pinch my lips not to laugh at his outfit. The big muscular former SEAL has on his typical clothes. They're the same he's worn the last two days, a pair of nice fitting jeans that make his butt look amazing and the company Pelican Bay Security polo shirt in black. However, what he has over it almost has me losing my fight with self-control. A bright pink — with frills on the side — apron covers his shirt down to mid-thigh. He's like my very own version of Mr. Mom, but cute.

The pan drips a few splats of water on the carpet. "I borrowed it from a friend," he says, shrugging when I can't take my eyes off his apron.

The hilarity of the situation is lost as I wonder what friend loaned him a pink apron. *Oh, shut up, Josie.* It's not like I have any right to him. It's probably from his gorgeous and skinny girlfriend.

Still, as Nate ducks back into the kitchen to finish what I presume are dishes, I take a seat next to Emma on the couch, propping my foot up on the coffee table and allowing my mind to wander. Have I ever been served breakfast in bed? Has anyone besides me loaded the dishwasher in my house? I know he's only here because he caught me feeling bad yesterday, but a girl could get used to this treatment.

"You forgot your post-breakfast snack," Nate says, leaning between Emma and me over the back of the couch. In his outstretched hands he holds an Oreo out for each of us. From the amount of white stuffing in the middle they're double stuffed — my favorite.

Emma is quick to grab hers and shove it in her mouth, eating at least half the cooking in one bite. She's never been one to turn down sugar. It takes me a few seconds longer. While I hesitate, he moves the Oreo back and forth enticing me to take it.

When I reach out and pluck it from his grasp, he smiles and pats me on the shoulder like I'm a good girl. It's a little demeaning, but I got an Oreo out of the deal so fuck it.

Emma eyes my cookie and snuggles a few inches closer on the couch so I plop it in my mouth fast. You can't hesitate with chocolate.

Nate brought me Oreos.

THERE'S a knock on the door and Nate jumps up from the couch where we spent the last hour and a half with the fictional doctor as she worked to heal all the broken toys in her neighborhood. I'm pretty sure at one point he hummed the theme song, but I decided not to call him out on it. The tune is catchy.

"Good, today's plan can begin." He walks to my door like he lives here.

I perk up. "Today has a plan?"

I've been under the impression the plan was survival until my boot comes off in a few weeks. Possibly for the next sixteen years until Emma moves out.

Nate smiles back before opening the door. "There's always a plan."

I agree, there's always a plan, but the problem arises when I don't know the plan. The last few surprises I received were nothing but horrible. I'm okay if I go my entire life without another one.

"Winnie, we don't want the baby to eat those," Nate says, and then the apartment door closes with him blocking my view of my neighbor.

She snorts. "Don't keep the woman away from cookies."

A few seconds later the bubbly blonde is in my living room hovering over the boot. "No one has signed it yet."

"No, they haven't." Probably because I'm not in high school and it's a black boot, not a cast.

"We can fix that later, Winnie," the friend my neighbor brought with her says standing beside her.

It doesn't take much contemplating to figure out which friend Nate borrowed the pink apron from. It's not Winnie because no woman in her right mind would dump the guy she's had in her apartment the last few weeks. He even came complete with a cowboy hat. I haven't been out and about to see if he's still coming around, but I imagine he is. It must have been the new girl with Winnie. Her long dark hair falls down past her shoulders and I smile back when she looks at me because it's the right thing to do. I try not to feel guilty for spending time imagining her boyfriend being in love with me, as though Nate wasn't here because I hurt my ankle but because he wanted to be here. This would be our normal lives, but with me up and moving. What does she possess that I don't? How come the cute ones always end up with hot guys and people like me get cheating Barry?

"Josie, this is Tabitha. She's dating Nate's boss, Ridge. Did you two meet?"

The vision of Tabitha being hit by a car is washed away in guilt. How could I even have such horrible thoughts about the wonderful person not dating Nate? Because I'm a bad person, that's why. It's the pain medication. I'm a woman in desperate times and all that.

"No, I don't think I have." I've met tons of people the last few weeks, so I can't be expected to keep all of them straight. Moving to a new town is tiring — especially a small one like Pelican Bay where you're expected to know everyone.

"Well, if you ladies are okay, I'll step out then?" Nate asks, his black baseball cap already stationed on top of his head. "I'll be back in a few hours."

"You're leaving?" The shock written across my face must be enough to show my displeasure because Winnie grimaces.

"We came to keep you and Emma company. Tabitha even brought cookies from the bakery."

The bakery serves the best cookies I've ever tasted. Definitely by anyone on the East Coast. I hate to see Nate leave, especially when he looks so excited to get out of my apartment, but if I can replace him with cookies, I suppose not all hope is lost.

"Go, do your thing," Winnie says shooing him out the

door. "Don't forget to stop at the police station before you come back," she yells as the door closes.

My eyes widen in question. "The station?"

Winnie and Tabitha grab quick glances at one another. "She doesn't know. Does she?"

Winnie shakes her head no.

"Have you had Anessa's macaroons?" Tabitha asks, passing over the large container of assorted colorful cookies.

I hesitate, still engrossed with the closed door as I wait to see if Nate will come back and rescue me. "Um, no."

"Oh my gosh you must try them. Katy says they are better than sex."

"Obviously she isn't doing it right." Winnie laughs, taking a cookie from the package. "Don't get me wrong. They're delicious, but nothing beats the other thing when done properly."

Tabitha nods like she understands what she's talking about, but as I take my first bite of the bright pink macaroon, I agree with Katy. I haven't had sex in over a year. And well, I've never had good sex... Ever.

Barry was more of an efficient lover in the bedroom. Get in, get the job done, and get out. The problem was sometimes he didn't complete the entire job. If you get what I mean?

"And what don't I know?" I ask. The macaroons are good, but I'm not that forgetful.

"Well..." Winnie looks to Tabitha, asking her what to do.

Tabitha doesn't appear to be any help as she stares back at Winnie with her eyes enlarged like a deer caught in the middle of the road between two cars. "I don't want to be the one to tell her."

Winnie cringes, not making the situation any better about whatever they need to say. "You're more involved than I am."

Tabitha sighs, pinching her lips together before she answers. "You heard Nate was almost arrested?"

4

"No? For what?" We may not be best friends, but I thought we had gotten friendlier the last few days. He didn't mention anything about being arrested. I even asked if he'd ever been to jail.

"Well, he almost ran you over with his truck." Tabitha nods her head, waiting for my response like this is obvious.

Okay, fine, it should have been. My mind has been full lately with work and taking care of Emma. I haven't put thought into what happens to someone who hits a person with his vehicle. But it can't be good.

"Ridge got him out of immediate trouble, but you could still press charges. You almost broke your ankle."

"No. I don't want to press charges." The thought never crossed my mind.

"Well, he needs to pay for any medical bills, and make him do a lot more crap around your apartment. Rearrange the furniture or paint something." Winnie grabs another pink macaroon. "Lift heavy furniture."

"It's the absolute least he can do. And the town will tar and feather him if he doesn't," Tabitha chimes in her opinion.

After a pause, I lean back on the couch, a small headache forming behind my left eye as it twitches. "I moved to Pelican Bay because I wanted to blend in with everyone else." I planned to find a nice little small town and set up shop and then keep to myself.

Both ladies laugh and Tabitha chokes on the maca-roons she'd been halfway through chewing. "You picked the wrong town for blending."

I nod, accepting defeat. "I'm starting to agree."

The police have not been by to get a statement for what happened in the apartment parking lot the day Nate hit me. Someone asked me a few questions while I was in the hospital, but I don't remember much of what was said because I was dealing with doctors and trying to figure out if my ankle was broken or not. The doctors still weren't sure at that point.

Although, this new information makes me analyze at the situation between Nate and me in a different light. Why is he here helping me? I hadn't questioned it all that much, thinking he was a nice guy who wanted to help take care of the situation he created, but is there another reason? Is he doing this so I won't press charges?

What kind of person is Nate? Is he a wolf in sheep's clothing? A man I let into my house because I considered him a good guy, but in actuality he's here for his own selfish purposes? Ugh. I hate the self-doubt my divorce created. I used to be so confident of my ability to make good decisions.

"IT's NOT that I don't want to live with Ridge, but I just feel like a girl should be married first," Tabitha continues thirty minutes later in our ongoing conversation.

Winnie rolls her eyes. "Tabitha, you haven't been to your own house in weeks. If you won't sell it, at least rent it to someone. You can make a ton of rent in Pelican Bay."

"You could. Property goes fast here, and it's expensive. That's why I'm renting outside of town." When I packed up and left Barry, I had to do it fast and there wasn't time to house shop. Now that we're in the apartment and I've been looking, either houses have offers on them before I get past the front door or they are way out of my price range. I was lucky to find the little fixer-upper I did. The one Nate saw on my laptop yesterday. Now I just need the bank to get their stuff in gear so I can make an official offer.

"The house has sentimental value."

My neighbor rolls her eyes again at her friend, and then shakes her head no at me, but I don't plan to get insert myself in the argument between the two women.

The apartment door squeaks — I need to put oil on the hinge or call maintenance — and all three of our heads shift in that direction. I could've sworn Nate locked the door on his way out.

"Honey, I'm home." He walks in the apartment smiling, a set of keys dangling from the door handle and a big smile on his face.

When did he get keys?

Who said that was okay?

Why does it seem like he and his friends railroaded my life the last few days and how can I stop it?

Do I even want to stop it?

As he struggles to pull his keys out of the lock with one hand, a large red and white pizza box flip-flops at the top of his other.

"Here let me help you," Tabitha says, jumping up to grab the box from Nate.

I frown, irritated that she gets to get up and help him so easily and I'm stuck in my chair fumbling around for a crutch — even if she has spent the last two hours in a nonstop poetic love fest discussing her boyfriend Ridge. I never had these thoughts about Barry. Was it a sign? A big one, which I missed.

Too bad I didn't listen to it when I had the chance. I have more feelings for Nate than I ever did for Barry, even if they are all mixed up right now.

"Hey, Josie, I got pepperoni. You're okay with that. Right?" Nate asks, looking at the other two girls. "Um, I'm not sure if I bought enough for everyone, though. If you give me a minute, I can go back."

Tabitha laughs, setting the pizza on my round kitchen table. "Nope, Winnie and I are busy. You two enjoy your dinner. Come on, Winnie," Tabitha says winking at her friend.

She doesn't waste any time and jumps from the couch like he poked her with an ironing prod. "Right, gotta go." She follows Tabitha out the door but turns back right before she leaves. "We'll stop in and see you again soon, Josie."

I wave. "Have a good evening," I yell, as Nate closes it behind their two retreating backs.

They sure left fast. The delicious aroma of cheese clouds my senses and I can't worry about them any longer.

"Where is Emma?" Nate asks, his eyes searching the living room. "It's quiet. Should I be worried?"

He is learning. I shake my head no. "She's taking a nap, but we should wake her up soon since it's after four. Otherwise she'll be up all night."

"Let me grab plates first and then I'll get her." The way Nate says everything makes it sound so simple. Like he's been here every day of our lives. Two people parenting together. I don't know what to make of it. Barry never even helped parent this way. He was more of a "tell me what I should do and then watch me do it" parent. When he was around, that is, which wasn't often.

"Come and sit at the table," Nate says, standing in the open space between the two rooms eyeing his pizza.

Right. Time to sit at the table with Nate, the man I've learned so much about while he's been absent for the afternoon. Winnie and Tabitha were full of information on my current home nurse — all of it good. Everything made my tummy happy dance at the thought of spending more time with him. It was an afternoon of feelings I'm not ready to have about anyone. Certainly not the man who hit me with his truck and is only here so I don't press charges against him.

"What did you do today?" I ask as my butt hits the bottom of the chair and I drop a crutch.

He shrugs with his nose crinkling up to match the corners of his eyes. "This and that."

I wish I could work out my feelings for Nate. Do I hate

him for hitting me with his truck? Do I think he's cute? Am I physically attracted to him?

I'm aware of the answer to the last two. They are yes, but I haven't worked out how I feel about what he's done to my life. It was already complicated, but he's added an extra layer by giving me an injury all because of his negligence. I should make sure he pays for everything just like the girls said.

Nate passes me one of the plain white plates I purchased before moving into the apartment — they were the cheapest ones at the thrift store — with two pieces of pepperoni pizza on top. I'm too lost in my thoughts to eat and instead pick at the crust, ripping off large chunks of the crispy bread.

"Is everything okay? Do you not like pepperoni?"

I rip off a piece of pepperoni hanging from the edge of one of my slices and pop it in my mouth. "It's fine."

"What is it then?"

"Nothing."

Nate narrows his eyes in my direction and taps a finger on the table. A few seconds pass before he opens his mouth again. "I hate the word nothing for an answer. There's obviously something wrong. Did you skip a pain pill?"

Well, then. His words piss me off faster than a bee sting hurts. Like the only reason something could be wrong with me is I'm cranky from being in pain. But he doesn't realize I'm still bruised and sore. And come to think of it, I did miss the pain pill, but that is *not* why I'm upset.

"I don't need a pain pill, Nathan." For whatever reason, using his full name makes it better. "I spent all afternoon wondering if you would come back and then you come in here carrying a pizza acting like everything is fine. Everything is not fine."

The left side corner of his lips tweaks up a smidge as he stares at his own pizza. By the time he lifts his head to answer his face is back into a calm unveiling mask. "I'm not leaving you, Josie. At this point you'll have to pry me out of here."

He says that now, but I've heard those words in the past. My ex once promised he never had eyes for anyone else.

I manage a few bites of pizza and in the process shred the pleated white paper napkin Nate brought in with the plates.

"Do you plan to tell me why everything is not fine or do you want to murder another napkin first?" he asks.

I ball the pieces up and shove them into my lap, my face becoming red. Why does he notice everything?

"Are you being arrested for hitting me?" I rush the question out as quickly as possible. His golden eyes glow in the faint light from the cheap chandelier over the table.

Nate blanches, leaning back in his chair. "Do you want me to be?"

Now it's my turn to not look in his direction as I answer. Do I? "No, but it makes me wonder why you're here. Is it so I won't press charges?" If that's the case he should know I won't, so he's free to go.

I glimpse his face as he shakes his head no. "If you want to press charges, I'll drive you to the police station myself. They're going to ask you for a statement anyway. I deserve whatever you do to me and more."

"So you're here because you feel guilty?"

"Yes," he says rolling his eyes. "But that's not the only reason why I'm here. Although I do have a selfish reason for helping."

I swallow and it takes more effort than it should. The dread of finding out the truth slides down my throat like a ball and plops into my stomach, causing waves of nausea. Why is it that I haven't learned to stop asking for the truth?

5

"I feel horrible about what happened, Josie, and I would be here making sure you and Emma were okay regardless, but the driving force pushing me is because I want to learn more about you."

"Me?"

"You have no idea. Do you?" he asks around a grimacing laugh, but he's the only one who gets the joke. "I hit you because I was staring at you when you were standing in the parking lot. I can't sleep at night knowing I almost hurt Emma and *did* hurt you."

"Excuse me?" How did he hit me if he was checking me out? "What?"

"I ran into you at the grocery store about three weeks ago. You didn't even glance in my direction. The day in the lot I saw you standing next to Winnie and I couldn't believe you were talking to someone I'd met. Small fucking town. My eyes were glued to you. I couldn't pull them away and then you ran right out in front of my truck. It was like my worst nightmare happening in slo-mo."

He takes a deep breath before continuing. I couldn't stop him even if I wanted. Which I don't. "You'll hate me after telling you this and you'll probably kick me out, but I need to get it off my chest. The guilt is eating away at me. Because I was stupid and wasn't paying attention and I could've seriously hurt Emma or you. I want to help you get well because I take responsibility when I mess up, but the selfish horrible part of me saw it as an opportunity to get to know you better, too. I am a terrible person and deserve to go to jail."

It takes me longer to figure out exactly what he's saying since I've been sluggish the last few days. The story still doesn't make total sense. Regardless, I believe Nate... likes me.

Wow.

At least he finds me pretty. How long has it been since someone admitted to almost hitting a woman because they were so taken with her that he couldn't stop looking at her?

"Why didn't you just talk to me at the grocery store?"

He smiles, shaking his head. "I tried, but you never even looked up in my direction."

"You could have gotten my attention and said hi." Thrown a pineapple or something. Nate is good looking, like hella good looking. He could have smacked me in the face with a piece of fruit and I would have gladly asked for more.

His smile grows but not necessarily in a good way as it resembles a grimace. "I hit you with my shopping cart."

"That was you?" I can't believe he's the man who hit my shopping cart so hard I thought he cracked my big jar of pickles. I'd been so furious. I'd almost told him off, but I was late to pick up Emma from daycare and didn't want to face the five-dollar-a-minute fee they impose when you're late. Plus Barry had called to give me crap about dressing Emma in too much pink and my mother wanted us to come for a visit. I'd kept my head down and scowled the whole way to the register mumbling about assholes with penises.

It's absurd, but as I picture Nate pushing his cart into mine in the middle of the grocery store and then hunting me down to hit me with his truck, I laugh. "Stop hitting me with things!" I yell with a smile on my face and toss my ripped-up napkin at his forehead. He catches a few pieces of paper an inch before they connect his face.

"Then start paying attention to me," he says back, a hesitant smile across his features.

"Momma!" a loud shrill comes from the bedroom. Emma is upset. She's never had a problem waking up before, but since moving into the apartment she'll get scared if she wakes up alone after a nap or in the morning. I'm hoping it goes away when she gets used to our new life.

Nate's laughter fades and he eyes my crutches with one perched against an empty dining room chair and the other on the floor. "I'll get her," he says jumping up and not waiting for me to offer. It's a good thing because I wouldn't have. I need to process a lot of things while he's gone dealing with Emma and I prefer to process them alone.

Less than a minute after he left the phone rings, and even though I hear it, I can't see the ancient cordless model I keep somewhere in the apartment. I would never have considered a landline for myself, but my mother insisted. She said it was for safety. So each month I write a check of wasted money to the telephone company. I didn't want to press any more of my mother's buttons than I did by moving so far away, so I agreed to get the service installed. But ever since then it's been a pain in my butt. Who even calls a landline phone anymore these days?

The phone stops ringing and I shrug, giving up on whoever had been trying to call — probably a telemarketer.

"Yeah, it's no problem. She's right here." Nate comes around the hallway corner with the phone clutched between his shoulder and ear with Emma resting on his opposite hip. Where did he find the phone? And what is he doing answering it for me? First keys and now this?

Emma reaches down to the floor, trying to get her dolls, and Nate puts her down before bringing me the cordless contraption I try to lose.

"Hello?" I ask. I hope he's smart enough to hang up on a telemarketer.

There's static on the other end of the phone and then the voice of my realtor cuts through so I can hear her. "Josie, I tried your cell first, but I didn't want to text this. I've got bad news."

That crappy clench in my stomach forms again. "What happened?"

"The little house you were interested in already has an offer. They offered full price and agreed to waive the inspection so the sellers took it."

My mouth falls open, distraught. "But I thought they said they'd give me and a week to get the paperwork?"

"I'm sorry, but there's nothing we can do. You didn't draw up the paperwork yet, and you didn't put any earnest money down to secure the spot."

"So that's it, then?"

A horn honks and I wonder where in the hell the realtor could be standing. There's never been this much traffic in Pelican Bay. "There are lots of fish in the sea, sweetheart. Every day someone lists a new house. We'll find you something. I've got to go. I have a showing but wanted to make sure you heard so we could resume the search. Your house is still out there."

The two of us share a quick goodbye and I hang up the phone, taking a minute to myself staring at my empty plate. I love my realtor, she's not much older than me and super chipper. She's a girl who was definitely a cheerleader in high school, but she's been around the block. She didn't love the house I wanted to buy. It's easy for her to say there are lots of other houses in the sea, but we both realize that's not necessarily true. Few houses come available in Pelican Bay and even fewer of them are in my price range. It could be months or even years before something else comes on the market. If I want to get Emma and me out of this apartment, we must look for something away from the cute little downtown area I fell in love with during my first drive-through so many months ago.

"Bad news?" Nate asks, sitting on the floor playing with Emma and her blocks.

I don't turn in his direction, worried if I do I'll lose the tight grip on my emotions. Forced to hold it together for so long already, I refuse to get upset about this. I'm not going to cry over it again.

"Yes, but I don't want to talk about it. Can you bring me a lot of Oreos, please?"

He stands and I don't have the heart to tell him the package he hid on the top shelf in the kitchen is gone. Fingers crossed he has other boxes stashed in the small apartment. "Can you get a glass of milk, too?" They're better dunked.

"Sure, Josie."

I'm eating the whole box so I can get fat and I can be on one of those shows the TLC channel runs. Where people are addicted to eating weird things. They could call me the Oreo girl. They'd probably give me a free package.

"HERE'S YOUR CUPPA TEA. Dipped not saturated to make the weakest tea I've ever seen," Nate says, passing over the large mug of light brown water. It took him a few days, but I taught him how to make the perfect cup of tea. I don't drink coffee, so it's my only go-to in the mornings.

I take a sip and let the warm water soothe my throat. "Thank you. It's perfect."

He smiles at the compliment. "You seem happier today. Feeling better?"

I take stock of my ankle and realize he's right. My spirits are higher. I no longer want to earn a free package of Oreos for being highlighted on TLC, so that's a plus. "Yup, I haven't even had a pain pill today. Before you know I'll be up and walking around all on my own."

"Let's not get too far ahead of yourself. You don't want to get back to normal activity too soon. It could re-aggravate the injury."

"Right. I didn't mean I was excited to do stuff. Just that I could." Ever since Nate's admission yesterday regarding the grocery store and his truck, things have been awkward. I'm not sure what to do. I don't have experience in this game. Do I tell him I like him too? That seems like the easy approach, but I didn't do it after our conversation yesterday and now the time for declarations has passed. His went by unanswered, making me a heel. The only way to tell him now is if I shouted it out randomly in the middle of a conversation. And considering the man has seen me cry, cleaned up toilet water from Emma, and searched through my underwear drawer to help me pick out clothes, he's seen me make a fool of myself enough for one lifetime.

I have to work it into a random conversation. The problem is that I'm the least smooth person you've ever met. I'm a highway the state hasn't paved since the Reagan years — full of bumps and potholes large enough to swallow a bus when you aren't paying attention.

"Have you heard from your office?"

I shake my head. "No, I left another message, but no one called back." I can fill out my time off paperwork online and I'm not in a super rush since I don't qualify for anything yet, but I'd be happier if I talked to someone. Maybe Nate will drive me over there in a couple of days. Let me get out of the house and smell fresh air.

In reality I should be ready to go back to work in a few days. I'm getting around with my crutches much better and as long as I keep my foot propped up during the day, I'll be okay. There's been no major swelling today. My bruises went from blackish to a weird green hue. I'm down to just using Advil as a pain pill. But I'm also in no rush because I fear that going working again means an end to having Nate around as often. If I'm able to work, why would he need to be here assisting me?

Watching the towering man was his tight T-shirts and his big open smile care for Emma are images I hope I've seared into my brain. He's so gentle with her. And me.

Yesterday, while eating dinner, she managed to get pizza sauce up her nose. I've been around the block once or twice, so I did my best to wipe it out and let it go. Not Nate, though. He took the time to make sure she was clean, letting her splash around in the bath for a good twenty minutes and then afterward cleaned up the gallon of water she'd sloshed onto the floor. Not once did he get mad or raise his voice—all things I'm guilty of doing at least once a day.

"Here she is," Nate sing-songs as he walks out of the hallway with Emma. She follows with her cute little wobbly walk a few steps behind.

At first I don't notice, but eventually I look up. That's when I spot the hair. Nate has mastered the top of the head ponytail and even managed to get pigtails almost in line, but everything else is way above his skill level. This morning he's attempted a braid, but only about a quarter of the hair had gotten in. The rest of her thin blonde tresses blow in the breeze created with her speed demon steps. Worse than the hair may be the outfit. Her afternoon attire consists of her adorable pink dress with a lacy bottom meant only for special occasions matched with a pair of fuchsia purple socks—the pair I keep meaning to throw away because there's a hole in the heel.

I cringe. Thankfully we aren't going in public today, but I appreciate his help nonetheless.

"Look, mama. Stocks," Emma says pointing to her socks, losing her balance and tumbling back on her butt.

"You look so beautiful." I clap my hands together once and wait until she runs over to where I sit on the couch.

"I'm gonna run to the hardware store and pick up the nails for the lock above the bathroom door. Do you want me to put her in her highchair so she is easier to watch?"

I level a steady eye on Emma and she looks up at me, smiling and giving me all the answers I need. I can't trust that expression. There's no way she'll give me peace while Nate makes a hardware trip.

"Let's let her rest in the pack and play." Emma hears and her face turns into a scowl. But once she's situated, I'll turn on the TV and she'll forget all about it. When I'm back on my feet, we're going back to TV-free days, even if I've learned to love the distractions.

"I won't be gone long," Nate says after putting a few toys in the play pen to keep Emma busy. "Do you need anything else?"

I don't, but my answer's stymied when he stops by the couch and leans down, almost as if he's a boyfriend giving me a kiss on the forehead goodbye. However, before his lips make contact he realizes what he's doing and pulls back. Rather than a kiss, he taps me on the shoulder as a friendly form of comfort.

I lied when I thought things couldn't get more awkward in this apartment. Nate needs to hear how much I like him before our relationship ends up in a place I don't want it to be. Like the friend-zone.

"No, I'm good. Thanks. Umm... We'll be here when you get back." I'm forced to yell the last part as Nate waves goodbye and rushes out the door as fast as possible, not looking back once. Damn it. Why didn't I just blurt it out when I had the chance?

In an attempt to keep Emma from causing any more expensive plumbing issues by flushing her toys, Nate agreed to install a lock above the bathroom door. I'm just hoping it won't cut into the security deposit when we move out. If I even still stand any chance of getting something back, anyway. He was all set to go until we realized the lock package didn't include nails and I don't own any. Nails for sure went to Barry in the divorce.

At least three minutes of silence passed as he stared at me trying to figure out why I didn't have a small container of nails in the apartment. I spent the same time staring back at him, wondering why he thought I would have any nails in my apartment.

Emma squeals in the pack and play and I turn on PBS, hopeful since it's still morning they'll air children's shows for younger kids playing.

There's a knock on the door. I groan when it doesn't open and I realize I must get up and answer it. Nate's in a lot of trouble for forgetting those keys he made himself. If he's going to hijack my place, he can at least remember to take them with him.

Using only one crutch — see I am getting better — I work my way to the door as soon as possible. I'm smiling, ready to laugh at the puzzled expression he'll be wearing afer he realized he got to his truck and had no way to start it.

"I can't believe you made me get up because you forgot your keys," I say opening the door as my mouth falls open and I'm left standing face to face with the last person I expected to see today.

My mother.

"Well that's not a way to greet your mother," she sputters already annoyed, which isn't a good sign.

I step back. "Hello, Mother. I didn't expect you." In fact, didn't I call and tell her not to bother coming because I had it under control? Why would she listen to me now when she hadn't all the times before in these situations? Why would she drive here now?

She pushes her way past me, much like someone trying to break and enter, and stops about five feet in scanning the apartment. "I told you I was coming to help."

"Yes, but then I told *you* I had everything under control." Twice. I told her twice!

My mother shakes her head in disbelief and clicks her tongue on the roof of her mouth. "And you always were a horrible liar, Josie. I knew there was no way you could get by without me. I'm only sad it took me so long to get here. I can see from the state of things you haven't been holding up well."

"If you had told me you were coming, I would've picked up more." I face the same direction she is and look around the apartment. Emma's blocks are on the floor and one bowl sits on the kitchen counter from breakfast this morning, but she can't see the other few items hiding in the sink. Given the situation, I don't think the place looks bad, especially considering I have done nothing in days and Nate does his best to keep us all up and moving.

"I told you I'd be here this morning." She doesn't waste any time and walks right over to Emma, almost recoiling when she sees the way her granddaughter's dressed.

We must have had this conversation on a day when I was still taking pain medication because I'm sure I'd remember if my mother said she was planning a visit. I would've taken action beforehand.

Like moved.

"Who did her hair like this? And the socks... You can't let her go public like this. What will the neighbors think?"

"We're not going out in public," I say once back in my spot on the couch, leaving the crutch against the arm rest.

If I wasn't injured, and I cared more about what my mother thought, I'd be busy cleaning up the house as she ranted about what I'd done wrong. But I've heard so much of it since the divorce I'm building up immunity. Don't get me wrong, she still annoys the crap out of me, but I now realize I can never live up to her standards. The only person who lives up to Samantha's standards is Samantha.

"You don't have a candle burning. If the neighbors can't smell how much nicer your place is than theirs, then what's the point of living in an apartment?"

I roll my eyes but make sure she can't see. "My neighbors don't care if there's a candle."

"The hostess guideline does. Your home should always have a welcoming smell when someone enters.

Yours smells like..." She sniffs the air crinkling her nose. "Toilet water."

Good to see old age hasn't cost her any of her five senses.

"And my god, Josie, there are Oreos on the kitchen table. Getting divorced is one thing, but letting yourself go altogether is another. I refuse to sit around and watch you throw away your life like this."

I should've taken a pain pill this morning to prepare for the headache I will get after a few minutes with my mother. If only she had warned me, I would have refrained from answering the door and spared us both the trouble.

"I doubt a few Oreos will be the demise of my life, Mother."

She clicks her tongue again. "That's what you think. A few Oreos here, and then you're eating pizza for dinner there, and before you know it, you're on drugs."

Please, Lord, don't let her see the pizza box of leftovers in the fridge. She'll have me in pepperoni rehab.

This is why I don't invite my mother over more.

"Is this the only bottle of Pine-Sol you have?" My mother peeks her head out of the kitchen, sloshing back a half-full bottle of brown liquid.

I nod. "Won't that be enough?"

I've only washed the floors once since living here, and the kitchen's not that big. The bottle should be plenty.

"It will have to do," she says going back to her job of scrubbing the kitchen floor.

By hand.

I'm sure she saw a crumb down there from the previous renters, but now she can go to all her friends back home and tell them how she saved my life by cleaning my kitchen floor. Thank god she's not on Instagram. She'd post before and after shots.

I will go insane soon if she doesn't leave.

It's been almost two hours since Nate went to the hardware store and he hasn't come back. I'm starting to worry he picked up word my mother is here and knows to stay far, far away. He's a deserter in my biggest time of need.

"Where's your required bottle of bleach," she calls from the kitchen.

I swallow, knowing she won't like my answer. "I use less abrasive products now that I have Emma."

It's not above my daughter's thought pattern to lick the kitchen floor, so I buy cleaning products that won't make me scared if she should get a small sampling. At least I try to use them when I clean, which isn't all that often, but no way in hell am I telling my mother that tidbit of information.

The door opens and closes as Nate comes into the apartment like he's running from something on the other side. "I'm sorry it took so long, Josie. The hardware was full of women and everyone was asking questions of Hank so I couldn't figure out where the nails were. I swear that place isn't put together in any logical order whatsoever."

Nate continues to rattle on, not noticing my open-mouth shocked-faced mother holding a bottle of Lysol standing at the edge of the kitchen.

"What is this? Why is this man in your apartment, Josie?" My mother stares at me like he's here to rob us. As if having a man near me is the worst thing she's heard all year. Obviously, she's forgotten the Oreos.

"Mom, this is Nate. Nate, my mother," I say, like everything is fine and the situation isn't crazy at all. I turn around and go back to the TV, trying to pretend that entire side of the apartment doesn't exist anymore.

"Well, what is Nate?"

Nate sputters. "I'm her boyfriend."

I whip my head back around, trying to give him a "what the hell are you doing" look, but his smile is as large as the Cheshire cat. He must think it's another fun game like the one he played with Barry, but he's never met my mother.

She leans her head back and laughs. "Josie would never date a man who wears jeans."

Everyone's eyes fall to the dark-washed jeans that hug Nate's legs and ass so well. I swear even Emma takes a second to admire. I don't know where my mother gets her crazy ideas, but Nate and a pair of jeans go together like peanut butter and jelly.

"Mother!" It's one thing for her to make ridiculous comments when she's alone, but not in front of someone — especially Nate.

But as usual he doesn't act the way I expect him to. Nate's smile gets bigger as he saunters over to the couch and leans down over the armrests, giving me the biggest kiss I've ever experienced.

His lips are warm and after the first second passes, where I worry he'll pull away but he doesn't, I grab onto his shirt getting him closer. The sensation of him against me warms my body, and my heart stops beating, trying its hardest to remember each and every second of this moment together. It's a kiss unlike anything I've ever felt — one of those kisses you know you can only experience once or twice a lifetime. One I never want to end. If possible, I'd spend an afternoon kissing Nate. His breath fills my empty soul as his lips move over mine with sweet possessiveness.

But as all good things do, this kiss ends when my mother clears her throat loudly. "Excuse me," she says before going speechless.

I laugh. I've never seen her wear her current expression in my life. This will be a story for her friends back home. Her face looks as if she's taken a shot of whiskey while sucking on a lemon.

"Just in case you were wondering, that was for real," Nate whispers in my ear before he straightens and stands next to the couch.

My eyes widen and I mouth the word, "What?" But he doesn't answer.

IF YOU HAD ASKED me two days ago what I thought of couples who were lovey-dovey, I would've made a gagging sound and told you they were the worst. I would have been wrong. They are the best.

Over the last few hours, Nate and I have thrust ourselves into the most over-the-top sweet and loving couple I've ever seen. I'd say you couldn't make this shit up, but we are. It's all natural.

It's wonderful to see the look on my mother's face.

Best. Day. Ever.

"Here's a glass of water to take your pill," Nate says handing me the glass with just a few inches of water and a pain pill. "Is there anything else I can get for you, snookums?"

I smile widely while taking the glass. "No, thanks, lover."

From behind Nate's back I watch as my mother rolls her eyes, thinking I can't see her. If she does it too many more times, they're liable to stick that way.

He stops for a second, staring into my eyes smiling. It's the new trick we've started, which evolved throughout the day. The prolonged silence and intense stare are driving my mother insane. Every time we do it, she huffs and I have to stop myself from laughing out loud. It's all fun and games now, but if she figures out we're messing with her, there will be hell to pay.

Until then I'm relishing how much I love playing house with Nate.

My personal hot man walks back into the kitchen with my empty water glass, and my mom huffs, standing up and brushing a few invisible lint pieces from her pants.

"Since you've moved on from Barry so quickly, I don't know why I'm here."

I don't either, I say, but only in my head.

"I'll give Emma a bath." She picks up the clean child from the floor and straddles her on her hip.

I smile. It makes me a horrible person that I'm doing this to my mother, but I can't help myself. "Would you like Nate to help you? He's got bath time down pat." Lies.

My mother scowls and I secretly laugh as she refuses

the offer. Nate has no clue what he's doing when it comes to bath time.

"No, I have it under control." She and Emma stomp off to the bathroom and I'm left hiding a giggle under my breath.

Tomorrow I'm sure there will be guilt for how upset she is, but she's being rather ridiculous. What mother is upset her daughter found happiness? Frankly, if this thing with Nate were true, I'd be pissed.

The room heats... Or more so it smells hot. Like someone left a curling iron on a little too long.

"Nate?" I call to the empty living room, hesitantly standing.

There's no response, and so with a single crutch I walk into the kitchen where I find Nate bent over the open oven. A few tendrils of smoke rise to the ceiling as he pulls out a pan of blackened cookies.

"Oh no," I say watching the smoke rise higher and higher. "Get the batteries out of the smoke alarm. Quick!"

Nate listens and, without having to use the chair, grabs the alarm from the kitchen wall and dislodges the batteries. The alarm makes a small beep, but it's more of a warning the batteries are out than an alarm over the smoke. I think he made it in time.

"What are we going to do with these?" he asks, hitting one a cookie with the spatula. It doesn't dislodge from the pan.

He looks so crestfallen, like these cookies were his life's mission. I can't let him go down without a fight. The man's a saint. He can't lose his mojo over burnt chocolate.

"Let me find my cell phone and I might have an idea. Hide the evidence and keep the oven on warm."

6

The smart phone, my link to the outside world, balances precariously on the arm of the couch. It only takes a few quick text messages with Winnie and we have a solution to the problem on the way. Having a friend who works at the bakery comes in handy.

The metal spatula scrapes against the pan as Nate does his best to chip away the blackened cookies hiding in the kitchen trash while I stare at him from the entryway.

It makes me stupid, but I can't help the way my thoughts are changing for Nate. The first few days he was an intruder into my home driving me insane, but there's this other part of him. The sweet part. I know the way we've been acting as a couple today has all been a show for my mother, but a part of me wishes it were true.

I'm worried I'm falling in love.

Which is absolutely ridiculous. First, I promised myself I'd never fall in love again. Second, I've only known the man like a hot minute. He could still be a serial killer and I wouldn't even know. Third... I don't have a third, but I'm sure I'll come up with one, eventually. There must be something wrong with him.

I lean against the thick archway of the kitchen and realize for the first time in a few days my ribs don't ache with the sudden movement. I'm feeling better. A lot better. I'll also need the crutches for my sprained ankle for another week, but the bruising in my ribs and knee is almost gone. The skin is an ugly yellow color, but I no longer have much pain at all. If I was a better woman, I'd tell Nate it's safe to go home. I won't press charges and I can get along on my own at this point, especially with my mother here.

But I don't want to let him off the hook. I don't want Nate to leave. Even if that makes me the most selfish person in Pelican Bay, I want more time with him.

A loud squeal seeps out from the bathroom followed by a harsh, "Now, Emma," from my mother and the smile I had while watching Nate fades.

"I'll go distract my mom," I whisper just in case she still has bat-like hearing. "When the cookies get here, put them on a cookie sheet and pop them in the oven so they're nice and warm when you pull them out."

My mother won't get over the fact Nate knows how to make cookies nor the fact that I'm eating sugar.

Nate smiles and leans down, kissing me on the forehead even though my mother isn't in the room. "We make a good team, snookums."

He's right. We are a great team together.

One I'm not ready to quit yet.

∼

"DON'T RIP out the cabinets! They're fine!" What is this woman thinking? She could paint those and they'd look brand-new. This decision will kill her budget.

The TV show cuts to a commercial break and the reality of my situation sets in like a sinking brick. It's a Saturday night and I'm yelling at the television while watching a show on HGTV. And the worst part is my mother isn't even here. She left two hours ago when Barry picked up Emma for his weekend visitation and I haven't changed the channel. After spending fifteen minutes cleaning the top of my stove, she said there was no point sitting around wasting the evening with me if I wouldn't even talk design with her. She made it two whole days with Nate and me faking a relationship — much longer than I expected. The person I sympathize with is my father. He went from thinking he had a fun bachelor Saturday night planned to having to entertain my mother and her outrageous expectations. A piece of Oreo falls from my mouth and lands between my boobs, forcing me to fish it out.

It's high time I face the facts.

My life is a mess.

I need to make some changes and get things in order.

But first I need more Oreos.

Since boob Oreo was the last in the house and I can't watch another would-be house flipper mutilate her budget buying overpriced kitchen cabinetry, the only option left for me is bed.

With a quick flick of my finger I'm able to turn the

television off and I groan as my muscles ache when I stand. Another sign of my impending age.

I've almost hobbled all the way to the bedroom when my phone dings with a text. My heart pounding in my chest, I open it as fast as possible, worried something happened to Emma, and she's been rushed to the hospital. I hate not having her in my direct line of sight.

With a sigh of relief, I see the name displayed across the screen, but then I pick up again in excitement.

NATE: Open the door.

That's a horrifyingly wonderful and scary as hell text to receive at 10 p.m. on a Saturday night.

I fix my hair into another — but not as sloppy — ponytail and toss my phone on the couch as I walk past it on my way to the door, the crutch slowing me down.

I'd like to play it off cool — because no girl wants to let on how excited a guy makes her — but there's no stopping my huge smile when I open the door and see the tall brown-haired Nate standing on the other side.

Thankfully, his expression matches my own. In his hands he holds a package of Oreos. My eyes widen and then raise taking in the strong line of his jaw all the way down to his muscled arms.

"You brought Oreos?"

It's like the man can read my mind.

He hesitates for a second, holding them out in front of him. "I did, but I'm not sure if you'll like them."

I narrow my eyes in his direction. Is this really Nate? Does he not know anything about me? "If it's an Oreo, then I love it."

He chuckles. "These aren't any Oreos. They're firework Oreos. They have pop rocks in them."

Pop rocks in an Oreo? Sounds adventurous.

"Apparently when you eat them it's like an explosion in your mouth," he says, the conversation turning awkward when I can't stop looking at his mouth.

I swallow as Nate's head gets closer to my own, the silence growing between us. I'm not sure what's happening, but I'm ready so I don't take the time to wait for him. Nate passes me the Oreos, but I use our close posture to wrap my arms around his neck and stand on my tiptoes, forcing our first official kiss. It doesn't take a pop rock for my mouth to explode from the taste of his lips against mine. He steps forward, pushing me into the apartment, and once clear closes the door with his foot. Nate backs me up against the wall and our kiss intensifies. His body surrounds mine, his skin and his smile make the universe fall away when I have his full attention. At the last possible second, I lean back gasping for air. Nate rains kisses across my chin and down my neck as I tighten my grip, bringing him tighter.

He cages me with his arms braced against the wall, and the air between us is thick with passion.

"We need to slow down," he says, lifting his head from the spot where he sucks on the sensitive piece of skin my collarbone.

"No," I whisper before tugging on the bottom of his ear with my teeth. "I haven't had sex since Emma was born."

Truth be told, I haven't wanted to since then. Things between my ex and me went south right after her birth and no one else has made me yearn to have that connection. Not until Nate roared into my life.

I step back, worried my admission will scare him

away. He ticks away at his fingers like he's doing math in his head and then stares at me as my cheeks redden in embarrassment.

I shouldn't have made that confession, but I found myself caught up in the moment.

"This can't happen here."

"What?" I ask, swallowing hard.

7

"**Y**ou need a bed and time to let me appreciate you properly."

He steps back and my arms fall away from his neck in despair. I don't need him to take his time. I need him to put his dick in me and give me an orgasm.

Nate basically drags me up from the wall, and I fight, not wanting to leave the space. As he passes, he steals the Oreos from my hand and throws them on the couch, not delicately at all.

I reach out, sad to see the chocolatey goodness leave.

When we make it to the hallway, Nate leans down, picking me up and wrapping my body against his. "Walk faster or I'll carry you," he says, as I cross my ankles, holding on for dear life.

I laugh. "I think you're already carrying me."

When we reach the bedroom, he drops my butt on the bed with a flop and my brain picks up where this is going.

"Wait, are you sure about this?" I ask, when I

remember what I have on underneath the grey pair of sweatpants I lumbered around the house in today after my mother left.

He raises his head, his eyebrows knit together. "Cold feet now?"

"No, but we could go to the bathroom for a minute." Or thirty. Put on some makeup.

He shakes his head. "There's no time for that."

"But you don't understand," I try again.

Nate shakes his head as he unties the strap in the front of my pants. "Yeah, you're fine the way you are."

"No really."

He leans back, his eyes searching my face. "Josie, from the moment I first saw you, I've wanted this to happen. You aren't going to take it back now because you think you're not enough or your underwear and bra don't match, or you want to brush your teeth. Whatever reason you've invented in your head. Trust me, whatever I find under here is going to be what I want. You are perfect."

Well, when he puts it that way. With no more complaints from me, I allow Nate to finish untying my pants and lower them until there's nothing between him and me except the black pair of granny panties I've switched to wearing over the last year. When you aren't expecting to get any, it's better to be comfortable.

Time slows as he removes my underwear from my legs, his fingers heating my skin as they make contact down my stubbled legs.

Nate tosses the underwear somewhere on my floor and then, with a hand wrapped around each of my ankles, he parts my legs exposing my flesh to the cool air of the room.

I swallow and lean back, resting my head on a pillow as he moves closer, the image too much.

"Watch me, Josie," he demands.

His head fits between my thighs and his tongue sweeps out, licking at my core. I moan as my eyes dart open, seeing the top of his head lost between my legs. With a groan, I squeeze my already spinning insides, my thighs shaking against his head as his dark brown hair rubs against my skin.

It's so warm, and when he blows a breath against my flesh, I arch my back up trying to get closer. I crave his touch as an orgasm grows in the pit of my stomach and gets larger with each tender caress of his mouth.

Two fingers stretch my walls as he pushes them inside my aching body.

"You're so wet. I love it." Nate moves his fingers, circling inside my core as my emotions continue to spiral. His compliments and admiration are more than I can handle.

I arch again, ready to come when he stops, pulling his fingers away. "Not yet, Josie. I want to feel you come around me the first time." He sucks on my clit and I arch closer, trying to pull a piece of an orgasm from his lips. "Not yet."

His pants lower and there's a tearing sound before Nate lines himself up and pushes past my opening without delay. I'm full, but ready, and after a few short pushes he's accepted by my body. He leans back moaning to the ceiling and lifts my ass in the air so he hits the same spot as before. Less than a minute passes before I'm back to the heightened point and I meet him thrust for thrust, wanting so badly what he's offered.

"That's it, babe. Fucking take it. Let go," he grinds out.

As if my body is already his, I listen, and my pussy clings to his dick vibrating with need around him as my orgasm releases. I bite my lip so I don't scream and scare the neighbors.

When my body relaxes, Nate lowers my ass and smiles. His eyes never leave mine as he pulls my hips getting himself deeper before he spills over, the jets of his cum stopped only by the condom and leaving me wishing there was no barrier between us.

"Fuck that was amazing," he says, slowing his movements but not leaving me.

My eyes close, lost in bliss as I nod in agreement. Is it always supposed to be that good or is it only because it's our first time?

"Are you sure I turned it off?" I do a quick injured ankle jog to the kitchen and see that, indeed, the oven is off. You can never be too safe.

Nate stands at the edge of the kitchen watching, a nervous expression on his face. "You checked the oven about twenty minutes ago. It was off then and we haven't cooked anything since, so you're safe."

"Sometimes the burners stay hot for a while." Fire safety is no laughing matter.

"Is there something wrong?" Nate crosses his arms against his chest and leans up against the wall as I hover my palms over each of the burners. "Do you need another orgasm?"

My hand doesn't get warm at all but my mouth falls

open while I stare Nate. "What?" Here he gave me two this morning. I've never had so much sex in my life. Even in my young carefree days when it's all I wanted to do. I don't know if I can handle another. I need time to rejuvenate. Do some Kegels or something.

"You are pacing. What's wrong?"

I drop my hand on top of the burner. Not warm. "There are only four hours until Emma gets home. What are we supposed to do without her when she's so close to getting home?" Doesn't he understand this is what parents do? We sit around and fret whenever left to our own devices.

"I can think of some things we can do," he says, lifting an eyebrow.

The implication makes a laugh. "No sex." Don't get me wrong, it was heavenly. I think I only slept three hours last night, but my baby is coming home and I'm already dressed now.

I should make her a cake — a welcome home cake. An I'm sorry you had to spend the weekend with your father cake. She likes chocolate.

"What are you getting out of the cabinet?" Nate asks.

"Oh." I close the cabinet door I just opened. There's no cake mix in there, anyway.

Nate steps into the kitchen and places a quick kiss on my temple. "You need some girl time. Let's go."

He takes my hand and practically drags me out of the kitchen. "Where are we going?" I ask without any resistance.

"To chocolate and friends."

Well then, all he needed to say was chocolate.

Nate drives me to the bakery and we almost make it to

town, the car passing the welcome to Pelican Bay sign with a wooden pelican sitting atop, when he asks.

"You think Emma will care if I spend the night tonight?"

He spent last night with me, but again we didn't do much sleeping. It's not Emma who gets a say. It's me. Do I want Nate to spend the night again?

I debate for less than a minute before I answer. "No, I don't think Emma would care if you spent the night. In fact, I think she'd like it."

Let's hope he picks up that I'm Emma. She's two. Unless he sprouted red hair all over his body and started talking like Elmo, she won't notice anything.

He slows the car when the speed limit lowers. "Do you want me to spend the night?"

I fight the smile that threatens to break, but lose. "Yes. I think I do."

"Once you decide if that's a yes or no, let me know." He smiles, pulling into a parking spot in front of the bakery.

He has to know I want him to stay, but just in case, I play along for longer. Not to string him along meanly but to build up the anticipation.

As soon as I open the door to the bakery, it's obvious something is off. Not only is there a charge in the atmosphere, but three girls behind the bakery counter jumping up and down and squealing in delight isn't something you see every day. Even at the bakery.

"Josie, look!" Winnie yells, grabbing ahold of Tabitha's hand and holding it up in the air like she just won a boxing match.

A hefty square diamond sparkles in the light from the

bakery. It's not the size of the ring that catches my attention, but what finger she wears it on.

"You got engaged?" The next thing I want to ask is to who, but everyone knows she's dating Ridge. There's no way he'd let anyone else close to her. Let alone with a ring.

"He did it last night, and I said yes."

"How did he ask you?" I walk over and inspect the ring closer. It's what you do when a friend gets engaged. I may not know her well, but I consider Tabitha a friend.

She reddens. "Um, that part is private."

My eyes widen and I look back at Nate, but he is sharing a moment with another tall guy wearing the same matching black polo shirt as him. They look at one another as if exchanging private communication, one that says "girls are crazy."

"You next, Nate?" his friend asks.

Nate widens his eyes and then narrows them on his friend. "Shut up, Crispin."

I slap him on the shoulder, but his friends only laugh.

"You wait, buddy. One day it will happen to you."

Crispin scoffs at the idea and crosses his arms as if he can protect himself in the women's presence. "The last thing I'm gonna do is put a ring on some girl's finger."

I step back and watch the excitement as Tabitha continues to show each of her friends the ring and each woman takes the time to admire the jewel. Just as friends should.

Memories cloud the moments as I remember what it was like getting engaged to my ex. There wasn't anything fancy about it. I knew he planned to pop the question. Barry wasn't ever very smooth. He asked my ring size, and when I didn't know, he took me to a store to get fitted. I suppose in the grand scheme of things it's what every girl should want. He proposed at a big family dinner with four generations in attendance. His mother, his grandmother, and even a great-grand-mother. She died three months later but was there to watch him pass down the family heirloom — a ring each generation of woman before her had worn. As her son married, she picked out a bigger prettier ring as a condolence prize.

Barry and I were the first people in his family to divorce. I often find myself wondering at night if he'll propose to his new bimbo girlfriend with the same ring or if our situation has tainted it and they'll have to start over with something new. Most of those thoughts stopped the day after his mother called me and explained that Lancaster men have a tendency for wandering hands, but you just have to suck it up and deal. In her opinion three generations of them didn't stay married for so long by getting divorced over the smallest indiscretion.

That conversation put a lot of things into perspective for me.

"Once you're married, he'll end up strapping a body camera to you." Winnie laughs at her joke, but Tabitha scowls thinking on it for a second and wondering if it's true.

"No, he's already bugged her phone with GPS. What more does he need?" Nate says, laughing as Tabitha rolls her eyes.

She shrugs, not denying the fact Ridge is tracking her cell phone. "He asked at the right time. And people around here have a tendency to get kidnapped."

Kidnapped? I look to Nate with her words, but he shakes his head.

"You got hit with a truck. Can you judge her?"

My eyes widen and I slap him with the back of my hand again. "*You* hit me with the truck."

He smirks. "It's an unconventional method, but it worked."

Only because my ankle is so much better and I'm ready to go back to work, I allow the joke to continue. Who laughs about hitting someone with a truck? What is wrong with people in this town?

"Did you have a good time?" Nate asks as he pulls back in my apartment parking lot.

After everyone finished admiring Tabitha's ring and she continued refusing to explain how he proposed, we celebrated with cake and I even purchased a piece to bring back for Emma. It's better than anything I could make from a Duncan Hines box.

"I did. Thanks for taking me." I've never been with someone who not only realizes when I need a little support, but acts on it to help me out. But spending the last few hours with friends in the bakery helped so I didn't miss Emma so much.

"What the fuck?" Nate asks, and I'm on high alert. My eyes scan the parking lot looking for whatever he sees.

Barry, with his hair gelled back, knocks three times on my car window, a scowl across his face.

I check the clock radio seconds before Nate turns off

the car. We still had forty minutes before he was supposed to drop off Emma.

He steps back to get out of the door, and before my feet are even settled, he's passed Emma to my waiting hands.

"Where have you been?" He spits the question at me in disgust, as if he'd been waiting around for an entire day.

Emma looks at her dad, scared. She's never liked hearing him yell. Nate tenses beside me and I worry what will happen if I allow these two men to stand off in the parking lot. Thinking quickly, I pass Emma over to Nate to occupy his hands.

"Can you take her upstairs?" She shouldn't see her parents fight.

"Josie?" he asked, his eyes wide with displeasure.

"Please, Nate." I can handle Barry. I've been doing it for years. But I don't want Emma to see him lose his temper.

I place more weight on my hurt ankles to keep my balance as Nate walks with Emma to the apartment door. A small tingle of pain coils itself around my ankle, and it's the first bout I've had in the last few hours.

"Well?" he asks again, but I've already forgotten the original question.

I cross my arms. Screw him. I'm no longer the sad little girl who got married too young and puts up with his bull crap. "Why are you here so early?" He never drops Emma off a minute earlier than he's ordered. I swear he used to drive around the block making sure she didn't make it back a second earlier than I wanted her.

"Where were you, Josie? Did you spend the night at his place?"

My mouth drops open, mostly because he has the audacity to ask that question. We're divorced. "No, I did not sleep over at his place." I leave out the part where he slept at mine. I've never been to Nate's house, and I get lost in the small moment thinking I need to invite myself over and see where he lives.

I must make sure he is not hiding a secret family somewhere. Not that I expect him to be that kind of guy, but I also didn't expect it of Barry either. I used to think he was too honest to keep secrets. Ha.

"I don't like Emma's mother out running the streets."

"Excuse me?" What street does he think I'm running around? "Is Pelican Bay a dangerous town in your opinion?"

He has no concern over what I'm doing. He's only pissed because he thinks I'm having fun. Barry doesn't like the fact I'm seeing Nate. He's allowed to move on, but I never should in his opinion.

"You should concern yourself with raising our daughter rather than someone you're sleeping with."

When he gets out this outrageous, it's easy to ignore him. I roll my eyes and step to the side, ready to walk in the apartment. I can pick up her bag of clothes later.

"Don't walk away from me," he says grabbing onto my arm.

I rip out of his grasp. "You're only pissed off because I'm dating someone, Barry. At least Nate is of proper age." He's older than me, rather than ten years younger.

The comment works as Barry hesitates for a moment before he stomps over to his car and retrieves the overstuffed diaper bag I packed for Emma. He practically throws it in my direction, and I'm forced to put more weight on my hurt ankle to reach out and grab it.

"Next time I drop her off, make sure you're here on time."

Next month it's my responsibility to drop her off and pick her up at his house per our divorce agreement, but I don't waste any breath telling him that because it won't do any good.

Barry has always only thought of himself and will always only think of himself.

THE NOISE from an electric toothbrush stops and the bathroom door opens, directly followed by a tall, ridiculously gorgeous man walking out with his hair dripping wet. Drops of water glisten in the light and as they drop to the floor, only a few are stopped when they hit the towel he has wrapped around his waist. Even though I'm positive I'm awake, I pinch myself to make sure this isn't a dream. Who thought me, Josie Summerton, would ever experience this sight in the flesh?

Nate smiles, shaking his head twice like he doesn't know why am staring at him — silly man — and then walks back into the bathroom to finish his morning routine. I'd volunteer to rub him down and dry him off, but I need to get myself together too.

It's a Monday morning and I should return to work today, but I haven't been able to get ahold of anyone at the office and my doctor's note covers me a few more days. So I'm stuck here spending time with Emma.

It's a rough life. Not.

I wish I could stay home all the time with her. At least for these few formative years before she goes off to school, but I need the money and a girl has to do what a girl has to do.

"I need to go home and get more clothes today," Nate says from the bathroom.

"I've never been to your house. I should go with you." My tactic is not subtle at all, but nothing between Nate and me has been normal.

He stops in his tracks, and for a second I worry he'll say no. But then he smirks. "A few more days and I'll take you home to meet my parents."

Nate drops the towel in front of me and the only thing that gets me through him dressing is that he has to go into the office today. They have a meeting he must be on time for.

We cannot have sex.

We most definitely cannot have sex.

Actually, I have no idea if Ridge's building is an actual office. I have serious trouble picturing Nate sitting behind a desk typing at a keyboard while pushing a thinly framed pair of glasses up higher on his nose and tucking his pen into a pocket protector. It's very unlikely any of that goes on when he goes into work. Plus he doesn't even wear glasses. He didn't tell me what work he had to do today, only that Ridge called a meeting, and he needed to be there.

It's so weird to be spending time planning my day with a guy again. I mean we broke out calendars last night and wrote joint appointments for the next month. Nate had a lot of work commitments in his that he has throughout the week where mine is spend time with Emma, feed Emma, play with Emma, put Emma to bed, work. It's the gesture that counts. I've never aligned calendars before. It's weird.

And wonderful.

It makes me think this is what normal relationships are like. Two people talking and sharing their lives and time together.

I didn't even realize what I'd been missing out on in my past with Barry.

When Nate leaves the bathroom for the third time, he's clothed and my libido sighs in defeat. She never gives up full hope.

He plants a quick but respectful kiss on my cheek. "I hate that I'm leaving you all day today. If Ridge didn't make it mandatory, I would stay home."

"Nate, don't be ridiculous. My ankle is fine. See?" I say twisting my ankle in all different circles. Sometimes I think the guilt over the fact he caused the injury makes him a little extra crazy about it.

"I called Winnie to come and check on you."

I roll my eyes, but he doesn't even flinch. "Nate, I don't need a babysitter."

"She's not here to babysit you. She'll stop by to check in and see if you need anything. Plus I have my cell phone."

With annoyance, I roll out of bed, not happy about starting the day but willing to do what I need to do if it will ease his nerves.

"I feel fine, really. Look, I could dance a jig." I never took dance lessons in school, so I have no idea what a jig is. I try faking a tap dance on my bedroom carpet, but my ankle comes down weirdly on a step and I cringe.

"Yeah," Nate says, shaking his head and putting his hand against my elbow. "Don't do that."

"What? I could've been an Irish dancer." If he plans to make comments about my dancing, I have to stick up for myself.

He laughs. "I'll contact the Riverdance guys for you. Set up an audition."

I'm in too deep now and can only pray he's joking. "You do that. Of course, I'd have to be on the road all the time dancing and who would take care of Emma."

He kisses me on the temple, this one lasting longer. "I guess you'll just have to miss out on your dream."

"It'll be a travesty, but I'll do it for Emma."

"Yes, for Emma."

A door closes and I freak out for a second worried Emma is walking around the apartment letting herself outside. Nate goes on high alert, his body frozen, but then Winnie's voice breaks through and calms the storm.

8

"I'm letting myself in."

I walk out to the living room and find Winnie standing at the dining room table taking off her shoes.

"Oh, you haven't left?" Winnie asks. "Huxley left about ten minutes ago."

Nate steps behind me and passes off Emma to my waiting arms. She rubs her eyes groggily, not a morning person today. "Shit, I have to go."

He pulls on Emma's pigtail and gives us each a kiss on the forehead before almost running out the door as he grabs a set of keys from the kitchen table on his way.

"Long night?" Winnie asks with one eyebrow a little higher on her face and a smirk written across her lips.

I sputter and shake my head no. "We we're just talking."

"Uh-huh. Huxley and I did a lot of talking when we first met, too."

Emma reaches out for Winnie, and surprisingly she takes her without a second thought.

"If you will hold her for a second, I will get some breakfast around."

"No problem," Winnie says, bouncing Emma on her hip and talking to her in a baby voice. "In all seriousness, I'm glad you and Nate worked out. He's a nice guy."

"He is a nice guy," I agree.

"Sometimes Ridge's guys have a tendency to be..."

I peek out from the kitchen where I'm pouring cereal for Emma. "Over the top?"

Winnie smiles. "Yes, exactly. Huxley didn't work for Ridge before he came here, but he fits in with all them. They're all bossy."

I nod, glad to hear I'm not the only one experiencing a bossy guy, even if it seems that way.

"And if you're not careful, they will move right in and take over your life."

I pick my head up in the kitchen again. "You too?" I hadn't thought about it until she said something, but Nate's been here for at least the last three days and shows no signs of leaving. Even said he'll bring over more clothes. It's not that I don't like the idea. I'm fine with him staying here, but how did I get a live-in boyfriend?

And who will tell my mother?

I'll wait until Christmas dinner to drop that bombshell. She wouldn't let a little thing like me dating someone ruin her Christmas meal. Probably.

"They take over your life. Don't they?"

Winnie sighs. "Yeah, but do you want him to stop?"

I shrug, but we both know the answer is no.

"Katy's downstairs. She says Pearl is pruning the flowers in the pots on the side of your apartment," Winnie says trying to keep herself from laughing.

I don't know Winnie or Katy all that well, but one thing I can tell you is when you say you need something done, these two step into action. Less than thirty minutes ago I made the comment I needed to get to my storage unit and find Emma's baby book so I can put in her first lock of hair after I get it cut this month. I wasn't planning on being in the apartment this long, so I put the book in storage not thinking I'd need it. Now I don't want to get her hair trimmed until I have a place to put the first clippings. She's gone past the cute messy bedhead look to unruly. It was one offhanded comment and the next thing I knew Winnie said she'd messaged Katy, who was on her way. I said no because I didn't have a babysitter, but Katy called Pearl on her way and picked her up before getting here. Every office I've ever worked for searched for the synergy these ladies have together.

I've only seen the aging hippie around town a few times, but Winnie promised she could handle Emma. Called her spunky.

When the two of them get together with a plan, it's hard not to just go along with it. They get you swept away in the moment. Everything is an adventure.

Even if it shouldn't be.

Like this simple run to a storage unit to collect a baby book.

Another minute passes while we wait for Pearl and I contemplate how dead the flowers are in the pots down below. It's gotten to the point I don't pay attention anymore. The big overflowing flowerpots blend into the background when I walk into the building. Eventually, right as I'm in the middle of mentally calculating the number of pots she's cleaning, there's a knock on the door and Winnie jumps up to answer it for Katy and Pearl.

Pearl wanders into the apartment following Katy, her eyes sweeping the room in every direction. The long pink tie-dyed dress, which reaches her ankles, sways with her movements as she walks. Her hair isn't in the braid I've seen previous times but pulled back and put into a tight bun at the base of her neck. She looks a little more nanny-ish.

"This place reeks of sex," the older woman says as she stops in the middle of my living room.

My face reddens and I swear my heart skips two beats as I stare her with my mouth hanging open.

"Pearl!" Katy yells.

Pearl shrugs, causing the pattern of her tie-dye to do a wave. "If the shoe fits."

"It doesn't. Does it, really?" I ask, stuttering over the words. My mother's candle trick is going first on my list tomorrow.

"No!" Winnie yells, staring at Pearl as if she doesn't know who she is or how she got into my apartment.

Pearl slaps me on the back and laughs, sounding a lot like a crazy old woman. We could stick her in a haunted house to scare all the children. "No, it doesn't, but now we know for sure what you and that hunk from Ridge's have been doing in your free time." She laughs again, continuing on as if it's the funniest thing she's heard all year.

I let out a sigh of relief, but my face stays red. Being sex smelly isn't something you want to be accused of, and I make a mental note to stop by the outlet stores on the way back from the storage unit to pick up a wall plug-in. Or five.

"Okay, out with you all. Go, have your girl fun time. I brought my radio in case I hear your codename on the walkie." She pulls out a huge, black walkie-talkie so large it takes up her whole hand.

Katy narrows her eyes in our direction. "What do you mean our codename?"

"You know."

Winnie shakes her head that she doesn't.

"The police give certain individuals monikers for use on the radio so they know who they're talking about without using names."

"Sure," Katy says. "But why would we have one?"

Pearl hesitates, her eyes flitting from one person to the next. "Well... you have a tendency to be talked about on the police radio."

I didn't think it possible, but Katy's mouth drops open wider until Winnie steps over and closes it with her hand.

"What exactly is our name?" Winnie asks, keeping her hand on Katy's chin so her mouth doesn't fall open again.

Pearl swallows and shakes her head a tiny amount like she doesn't want to tell us, but she opened this door and now she has to walk through it. "I'm not positive, but I think they've referred to you as The Bakery Bandits."

"What? That doesn't even make sense. Who started this?"

Pearl shrugs. "I'm not sure. It's been around for a while."

"A while?" Katy asks, stepping away from Winnie so she has use of her mouth again. "I'm so tired of the men in the state. I am moving far away.."

"You won't find that man sitting in this apartment so you best go do your thing. I'll keep my ear out," she says shaking the radio.

Katy turns around in a huff, mumbling something under her breath as she walks toward my door. "You won't need it," she yells back before stepping into the hallway.

The mumbling and ranting continue as Katy drives us to the storage unit. I sit my butt in the back seat and pretend to not understand what's going on. Truth is, I haven't been in Pelican Bay for long, but at times it's like I've lived here my whole life. I'm assuming there's a history.

"It's not that outrageous, Katy," Winnie says.

Katy's eyes widen, and she stares at Winnie like she's grown a third head. "It's outrageous. I'm always blamed for things."

"You ran your car in that cornfield senior year."

Katy scoffs like she can't believe Winnie has the audacity to bring that up. "That was an accident, and no charges were filed."

Winnie doesn't respond, but Katy continues to stare her friend down.

"Did you know about this?"

Winnie lifts a hand to her chest. "Of course not. I'm just saying stranger things have happened around here."

"I bet you this is Pierce's fault."

"Oh look, we're here," I say although we're still fifteen feet away from the turn off for the storage buildings.

Katy looks to the backseat, her attention no longer trying to silence Winnie with her laser eyes but instead focused on me although her expression changes to a smile. "Do you need help going through boxes to find it?"

"No, I remember right where the box is." It holds all my special memories from Emma so I didn't want it to go on the moving truck and instead brought it over my car. The box was one of the last things left in the storage unit. It should be super easy to find.

Winnie makes the turn to the parking lot, and I give her directions to locker 102 toward the back of the fenced-off area. It's not a huge storage unit, but it holds most of my belongings right now. When you think about how my whole life can fit in this little ten-by-twenty space, it's kind of sad. I can't wait to find some place permanent in Pelican Bay and grow roots here.

"Your neighbor's door is open," Katy says as she gets out of the car and walks to the open unit next to mine. The storage unit has its garage door wide open, but no one seems to be around.

"Maybe they had to go to the office for something," I say, stretching down to the ground to unlock my door. The key on my padlock always sticks and I'm forced to pull it in and out, jiggling it around before the padlock pops open.

Winnie stands behind me, blocking my light and watching me fumble with the lock. "Katy, you can't just walk into someone's storage unit."

"I just want to see what they have in here."

Winnie shakes her head. "Katy has boundary issues."

"Clearly," I pant, pushing open the heavy storage door.

"She doesn't always listen well either."

I need Winnie's help to get the door all the way up since I don't want to put too much weight on my ankle. "I haven't noticed," I lie.

"Um, guys," Katy yells, backing out of the storage unit.

Winnie stiffens and drops her hands, leaving me holding the weight of the door alone. "What?"

"It's full of drugs." Katy stands a few feet from the open storage unit, her eyes never wavering from the middle of the room. "A whole stack in the middle."

Winnie walks over to Katy without getting close the door and does her best to peek inside. "What is?" she asks as if she doesn't believe her.

I forget all about Emma's baby book and join the pair while not getting too close to the open unit.

"All those banana boxes are full of white stuff wrapped in cellophane." Katy points at a stack of banana boxes nine or ten high sitting in the middle of the storage unit. The rest of the area around it is empty.

"How do you know what drugs look like?" I ask.

Katy looks at me like I'm the dumb one. "I watch TV. Haven't you ever seen *Scarface*?"

"Are you sure?" Winnie asks, her voice filling with panic. "Huxley will freak."

"I swear. One a lid was off on a box in the back."

"Why the hell did you walk to the back?" Winnie yells and I panic.

I grab both of them by their upper arms and walk them back toward my unit. "What are we going to do if they come back?" I whisper.

Both women pause as if this is the first they've thought of it. Let's be real. You don't leave boxes of drugs in a storage unit with the door open and not expect to come back. Quickly.

"What do we do?" Winnie whispers, fidgeting with her hair as we all huddle over a box in my unit. That way at least if someone walks in, we won't look suspicious.

"We need to call the police," I say, like the only logical person in this room. What else would we do?

Katy grabs on to my arm with a death grip, her fingers pinching my skin. "No! We can't do that."

9

"Why not?" I ask.

Her eyes widen and she pleads for something with them, but I don't know what. Drugs go to the police. That is the rule. "My reputation can't handle it. We're already known as the Bakery Bandits. What will Pearl say?"

I roll my eyes, but when I get a flash of Winnie, she seems concerned too.

"Huxley will never let me hear the end of this. We need to call somebody and get a handle on this situation."

"You guys, there's a storage unit full of drugs. We need the police."

"No," Katy says, her eyes now bright. "I have a plan. We'll call Tabitha."

"Tabitha?" I ask, confused. What does she have to do with this? Are they smuggling drugs in the bakery? It would make more sense with the name, but I can't see Ridge dating a drug smuggler.

I'm clueless, but Winnie nods her head like she's following along. "That's a good idea. We'll take the drugs and put them in the back of the car and drive them to Tabitha. She'll know what to do."

Okay, now I'm starting to worry. What is happening at the bakery downtown? Who am my becoming friends with and why would Tabitha know what to do with a storage unit full of drugs?

"Okay, but we have to work fast so we can get the drugs loaded before anyone comes back."

"You guys are crazy. You know that. Right? We should call the cops. That's what they do." Police handle drugs. It's in the job description.

"No, it's not. If we call the police, my cousin Anderson will show up and it will be all over town. He loves rubbing my face in it when this kind of stuff happens."

"Do these things happen to you often?" I whisper leaning over the box of dishes we're using as a decoy. If this has happened before, she does need a codename on a police scanner.

She shakes her head. "That's not important. Pop the trunk."

Both women bump fists together and walk out of my storage unit, leaving me standing alone, shaking my head and wondering when we all agreed upon the fact that we're putting drugs in a car and to drive to the bakery downtown.

When I don't move right away, Katy pops her head back in my unit. "Come on, Josie. Close this thing up. We have to move."

She says it as if this is absolutely an everyday normal kind of thing. Like today is Wednesday, we load the car up with drugs and drive around with them. When did I get dropped into the Twilight zone?

I have a mini panic attack and clutch over in the middle of my storage unit trying to regulate my breathing so I don't have a heart attack and die right here breaking up a drug stealing operation. By the time I make it outside the storage unit, Katy and Winnie each carry a covered box with the image of bananas on the side. The trunk of the car is down and both women put their boxes in the back seat.

I run over to the car freaking out. "You didn't put them in the trunk?" I ask when I see the backseat has four boxes on the floor and seats. Katy turns back to grab the last one from the storage unit without giving me a second of notice.

"The trunk wouldn't hold them all," Winnie says like that's obvious.

"I'm not riding back there with them." Are all these women crazy?

Katy opens the back door and shoves the last box of drugs on the seat. She misses, hitting the box on the side of the car, and a rectangular-shaped white brick slips over the top of the box and falls on the ground with a thud so loud I worry someone will think it's an explosion.

"Shit." Katy scrambles to pick up the bag, but as she does, white powder falls from a new hole created on the end from the fall. "I'll ride back here. Hurry. We need to motor." Katy tosses the leaking bag on the car floor and sits down next to the stack of boxes.

Winnie slams her door and then jumps in the driver's seat starting the car while I climb into the passenger's seat, not at all sure what we're about to do. The car charges off with a lurch and I'm still buckling my seatbelt by the time we make it out of the storage unit parking lot.

"Slow down," Katy directs. "We don't want to get pulled over."

"Yes, please slow down. That's the last thing we need," I plead as Winnie reduces her speed and heads to Pelican Bay, each of us pretending we aren't driving around with a bunch of stolen goods. Stolen drug goods.

The twenty-minute drive to Pelican Bay proper gives me a lot of time to contemplate my choices in life. I'm not sure how I ended up here, riding with two women in a car stuffed with drugs, but I feel like at some point maybe I did something wrong. Maybe I ate too many Oreos. Maybe I didn't eat enough Oreos.

If I was a home eating Oreos right now, I wouldn't be in the car full of drugs.

"Don't worry," Katy says patting me on the shoulder as she leans up front from the backseat. "We'll make it to Tabitha and she'll take care of everything."

"Does Tabitha sell drugs?" I ask the question I've been holding in since this crazy thing started.

"No!" Katy yells, startling Winnie. She reduces her speed again as we get closer to town. "She's wholeheartedly against drugs. But her fiancé Ridge will know what to do."

"So you plan to drive a car full of drugs up to the bakery and then what? Tell her to call her fiancé over and get the loot?" How will this not cause us trouble?

Katy taps a finger to her chin. "Well, when you put it that way, maybe we should have called him from the storage unit."

My eyes widen and I have to focus on my breathing as my heart thumps in my chest. "You think?"

Nate works for Ridge, and while I don't know the man, I can't imagine how Nate would respond if I called them up and told him I was riding around in a car with drugs. In fact, I can guarantee it would not go well. None of this will go well.

The car hits a pothole and the box on the top of the stack next to Katy wobbles and tilts toward her. She braces the stack with an arm, managing to keep it up.

"Whoops," Winnie says, turning the car with a hard left as we get closer to Pelican Bay. The stack of boxes hits the window and Katy hugs the middle one trying to keep everything lined up.

"Shit, we've almost made it," Katy says as we drive past a cop car stationed on the side of the road using a radar on cars as they pass. She smiles and waves as we pass the police car and we all breathe a sigh of relief when it doesn't pull out into the road after us.

"I will need so much church for this," Winnie says, stopping the car in the back parking lot of the bakery.

"I just can't believe you did it," Nate sputters in complete disbelief.

It's been four hours since we dropped the car load of drugs off at the bakery and left Tabitha with a bunch of similar questions. Anessa, the smart one, refused to let the drugs enter the store. But eventually, without even being called, Tabitha's fiancé and a few guys showed up in the back room, and magically the drugs disappeared.

Ridge put the three of us back into Winnie's car and told her to take me home.

He kept calm, but it was one of those calms where you know it's fake. There could have been smoke coming from his ears if the bakery wasn't so warm.

I have a feeling I won't be hanging out with the Bakery Bandits again soon.

"Whose idea was it?" Nate asks, pacing my tiny bathroom as Emma splashes in the tub unaware the trouble her mother got into today.

"Well, it kind of just happened... a little Katy." But I hate to put all the blame on her. We followed along. Winnie didn't object either.

I'm not sure what happened to the drugs. The tall guy named Bennett promised us Winnie's car would pass a drug inspection and not to worry about it. Not that I think she has one of those planned anytime soon. He then promised all of us to secrecy and told us to pretend like it never happened. After that he called some guy named Spencer and told him to wipe the video surveillance. It had been more than a little shady.

Nate paces a few more times, mumbling under his breath. The name Katy is the only word I make out on a random occasion.

"Do you know all the stories I've heard about her?" he asks, when he finally stops for a moment. "If I had believed for half a second, they were true, I wouldn't have let her in the apartment."

"Wait!" I say squeaking a little rubber ducky at Emma to keep her distracted. "Katy is nice. You weren't there, Nate, but the situation was stressful. We had to act fast." It's true.

I'm not happy with how it went down. If we had been pulled over and arrested for drugs before we made it to the bakery, life would have gotten bad. Custody of Emma would have been in question and I could have lost her. Barry would never let me near her again if that happened. On the ride back to my apartment I vowed to make smarter choices from that moment forth. At the time it didn't seem so horrible. Well, that's a lie. It was a bad idea from the start, but Katy was persistent and I was so scattered. Everything happened so fast I had to go along with it. Winnie agreed too.

"Do you know the local police station calls her the Bakery Bandit?"

I smirk, remembering the conversation from earlier in the day. "Yes, I've heard."

"Josie, I don't know what to do about this," Nate says, sitting down on the toilet and putting his head in his hands.

"Why you have to do anything about it? The situation is handled." Sure, it was a stupid decision, but the result was the same. The drugs are in Ridge's hands now. And no one will be the wiser about what happened.

Nate shakes his head. "You don't understand. This stuff always has repercussions."

Emma splashes her hands in the tub and then her little body lurches over and the worst baby olive-green vomit projectiles out of her mouth like my child has been possessed by the same demon who stars in the *Exorcist* movies. Green goo covers the front of the bathtub and I reach into the water getting the second round of puke all over my arm. The water turns the most disgusting shade of green and I gag, grabbing her out of the tub while splashing the liquid on the floor.

"Oh my gosh, Emma. What happened?" I ask, searching the bathroom for a towel.

Nate jumps up from the toilet with a towel in one hand and takes Emma from me, wrapping her up. "Drain the water from the tub and then use the shower head to wash it out. I'll clean her up with a wipe and put her in some pajamas in case she throws up again."

He marches Emma out of the bathroom, leaving me to deal with the sticky green cleanup as he sweetly talks to her in a calming voice about how she's going to be okay and that he's got her.

My heart melts at the situation — a moment of happiness mixed in with worry over my daughter and trying to remember where I stashed the thermometer the last time I needed it. All the happy feelings disappear when I turn back and see the spreading green glop as it takes over the rest of the clear liquid in the tub. How did I get stuck with this part of cleanup?

"Don't you need to work this week?" Nate asks, leaning over my bed and lacing his black chunky work boots he wears every day.

I lie back on the bed, readjusting my head on the pillow as I pull the covers up around my shoulders. "No, I got through to my boss, but he said the temp worker who replaced me is scheduled for the week so I could take another one off." There isn't money in the payroll for us both.

Honestly, I was a little upset at first when he told me they didn't want to take the hours away from my temporary placement, but my doctor's note covers me for the rest of the week and I've enjoyed being able to stay home with Emma. You miss out on so many little things during the day when you're working. My ankle is feeling better than even I expected, and by next week I'll be ready to go back. Plus, Emma will feel better by then.

"What are you doing at work today?" I ask him every day but he never tells me.

He did tell me he'd have to run a few "trips" this week. He didn't elaborate on what the trips were, and even though I'm dying to know, I'm doing my best not to ask. We're a hot minute into this relationship. I don't want to become the crazy girlfriend all up in his business.

There's a small thread nagging in my brain and warning me that I should worry his trips are to a secret wife or prettier girlfriend, but I work to bash the horrible thoughts down to the far reaches of my brain. Nate doesn't seem like the cheating type. Plus, I'm sure you have to be with someone for more than a week before they're allowed to cheat.

I'm perfectly aware I have trust issues after the divorce — I gave a therapist a lot of money to tell me this many times before I believed it — but I didn't expect them to show their ugly heads so soon. There's a small possibility I'm not as grown-up, mature, and rational as I once believed.

I watch him bend over to tie his other shoe, the muscles in his back stretched across his bare skin enough to make me wish we could stay home and lie in bed together all day. But then Emma cries out and he stands, promising to get her.

Great muscles and he takes care of a child. Could any woman ask for more?

Probably more than a crazy woman with trust issues who rides around in a car full of cocaine with two girls from the downtown bakery.

I have *got* to get my life together.

Starting today I will be the perfect mom and girlfriend. I'll even make some cookies. Cookies make everything better, damn it. I'll do my hair like my mom always says how it looks cute when I wear it half up and find a dress that makes me look matronly, maybe something a little 1950s era.

"Her head feels cooler, and she acts like she feels better today," Nate says, setting Emma on my lap.

I woke up with her around eleven, gave her more meds, and rocked her back to sleep. At two the sound of her shushed cries rattled me again. I felt my side and found the bed empty. Nate held her in his arms gently, pacing with her in the middle of her bedroom and whispering sweet nothings.

If I hadn't been so tired and ready to fall back to sleep right there on the floor, my panties would have melted off. Screw looking at half-naked firemen holding puppies online. All I need is a mental image of Nate being tender to Emma for the rest of my life. He might not know how to do her hair, and he's still unsuccessfully trying to teach her how not to fling spaghetti against the wall, but the man is amazing with a child who isn't his own. Better than her actual father.

"Hello, sweetheart," I coo and watch as Nate pulls on

a black long-sleeve shirt and covers his chest up with a sleeveless vest. It might be Maine, but it's the middle of the summer and he's never dressed in layers before.

"What did you say you're doing today?" I try again.

He wrestles with putting a watch on his left wrist, not turning back. "A little of this, a little of that."

Fear, jealousy, and suspicion prick at my chest.

I will not go crazy and demand to know what he's doing today.

I will not go crazy and question him before he leaves. That behavior makes me a psycho.

I take three long breaths and repeat the mantras to myself again. Nate has given me no reason to suspect him, and I won't ruin a good thing because the asshole I married before screwed with our relationship and my brain.

"What's wrong?" Nate asks as Emma pulls on a tendril of my hair.

I work to remove her tiny little baby fingers that have gotten stuck between the strands and answer, "Nothing."

"It's never nothing when a female says nothing."

Do I lie, or be honest and let him see the crazy that is me inside?

"Is this about the job?" Nate asks, even though by the expression on his face he's already determined the answer is yes. Smart man.

I sigh, pretending like he's the crazy one. "Of course not."

"Josie, unfortunately with what I do, I can't always tell you what I do every day. It keeps you safe and there are confidentiality issues I have to deal with for certain clients," he says sitting back on the bed.

All those things are the truth. He's off doing superspy business or whatever Ridge's company does, but it's also a convenient excuse a cheater would use.

"I'm sorry, it's just with my past and how crazy I am."

He chuckles, kissing me on the forehead like I'm something precious. "You're not crazy. Look, I won't be able to be on my phone much today, but I'll let you track me."

My eyes narrow at the suggestion. "Track you?"

Visions of me sitting in my car, hiding below the window, and using the long scope on a camera to take pictures of him flash in my mind. I watched the show *Veronica Mars*, but it's not a career field I'm looking to get into.

"It's easy." He grabs his cell phone from his back pocket and gathers mine from the night table. He taps on the phones for a few seconds and holds them both on his knee. "I thought I told you to password protect this thing?"

"Emma likes to play the games." I have colors and letters learning songs on my phone for her. Before I had kids, I always said I wouldn't be one of those parents who stuck a device in front of my child's faces, but you know what? They work. You have a kid screaming in a shopping cart because you're taking too long to pick out what kind of broccoli you want for a side dish next week, and the only way to get them quiet and out of the store without causing a scene is a shove the phone at her, that's what you do. At least she's learning her ABCs.

"There, we're all set," Nate says, pressing a few more buttons on my phone.

He passes it back and then taps on the new green-colored square with a weird white design in the middle. "You tap on the app and the tracker will show you where I am."

"For real?" I grab the phone from his hands and the little map loads, showing a red dot and a green dot right next to each other.

"Promise you won't tell anyone where my dot is?" he asks, tilting his head to the side and giving me a look.

"Yes, I promise." I cross my finger over my heart.

Who knows why his actions mean so much to me? But they do. I stare at the green dot labeled Nate, reassuring me he's right next me even though I can see him as he sits on the bed. If I was younger and a little more naïve, I would tell my friends it was absolutely crazy. You don't attract someone with the issues I have, but I'm older and wiser. My heart has been broken. I'm aware that in life you clutch on to the little things that give you some sense of peace. And call me crazy, but knowing I can see Nate's green dot whenever I want is already providing me peace. Tabitha's not so crazy.

Just the fact he's willing to do it and thought of the idea himself is enough. I can't imagine Barry ever offering such a concession. Then I would've known when he was out to late night dinners with his girlfriend or visiting the small studio apartment he'd rented for her. I'd have found out about all those times he promised me he was working late at the office he was at a strip club downtown.

Nate pats Emma on the head and then slips off the bed. "I'll be back late. Don't forget we have dinner at Ridge's house tonight for a meeting."

"Dinner meeting? Aren't those for his employees only?"

Nate grins, his white teeth visible in his exaggerated smile. "After yesterday's trouble, Ridge has decided meetings include girlfriends and eventual wives from now on when they can."

"Are we?" I ask, too scared to say the word "dating."

Nate nods his head, shaking it once. "Of course we are and even if we weren't, you still have to go because I'm not letting you out of my sight."

"But we are, right?" It's fine if I want to triple check. Right? Get it in writing.

"Josie," he says with a hint of disbelief as he leans down and kisses me on the lips and then tugs gently at Emma's hair. "I wouldn't let anyone track my phone unless I planned to be with her for a long time."

"Oh," my face heats and breaks out into a smile, way too happy over the fact Nate just made me his girlfriend.

It feels so much like high school, but I don't care.

I have a boyfriend.

I have a boyfriend and he's hot.

"My phone will be on silent, but if something happens or you need me, text." He tucks his shirt in and heads for the door, turning back once. "And Josie."

"Yes," I respond, looking up from Emma.

"Don't leave the apartment." And then he keeps on walking right out the door.

Men.

"ARE you sure this shirt looks okay?" I ask, pressing down on the wrinkles I just noticed in the long pink T-shirt I put on to wear to Ridge's work meeting. The shirt is long enough to cover my butt because since having Emma I haven't quite gotten my ass cheeks to fit into a pair of jeans properly. I also have a baby, so there was never enough time to go jean shopping.

Nate stops walking, using a few seconds to grab Emma from my arms and bounce her on his hip. It's probably the safest choice because I'm not sure I should be trusted to hold the baby, walk, and get creases out of clothing while talking at the same time. "Baby, you look amazing. Stop covering up that ass. It's a sight to see."

I stare up, puzzled. "My ass?"

He leans back, staring at my rump, and then licks his top lip. "One day I'll bite it."

My eyes widen, a bit in worry and a lot in excitement. I wonder what that would be like?

"Josie! Over here," Winnie yells from the front door of Ridge's home before I get the chance to ask for more details.

"This won't be one of those parties where you abandon me to go hang out with your girlfriends. Is it?" Nate asks, smiling... so he's not upset about the possibility.

I nod. "Probably." And that's wonderful. I can't remember the last time I had more than one friend at a time. It seems crazy, but I belong to a group. I have friends with an *s*.

Nate holds the door open and Emma pushes her favorite baby doll into the side of his neck. Ridge's home is splendid. We walk up into the large two-story colonial home where I'd expected to see lots of wood in traditional features, but it's the opposite. I can still see some original features of the house, like a big strong staircase made of dark wood, but the rest of the home is modern with open spaces and large rooms. It's like every East Coast girl's wet dream of a house.

I gasp when we get to the kitchen. There's white and stainless steel everywhere with a long island separating the room and the countertops glistening. They're all covered with dishes others have brought. A few store-purchased items are mixed into the lot with homemade options right beside them.

Nate drops the bag of potato chips we brought, our lackluster combination looking very pitiful next all the covered casserole dishes. I'm just impressed he'd been able to handle Emma and the chips with neither one of them ending up flattened. He's only been helping me out with Emma for a few weeks and already I feel like he's better at this whole parenting thing than I am at times.

Nate's height puts Emma right at Tabitha's eye level, and she gets as close to her face as possible, talking in all the cute baby terms about how adorable she is. Emma stares at her and then looks at me as if she's had enough and it's time for me to remove her entourage.

"Nate, you can go out with Ridge and the other guys in the yard. We'll take care of Emma."

Nate eyes Tabitha skeptically. "I'll take her with me," he says bouncing Emma a few more times as she smiles and laughs. My child loves him too. "You want to watch the grill. Don't you?" he asks, and her little face perks up into a smile.

Tabitha looks to me for help but I only shrug. What can I say? Emma likes the man.

I watch as Nate walks out the door and notice the smattering of men in the backyard. Ridge has a large deck with a grill set up on the side, and two men hover over the area. Beyond that, in the huge green space of his yard, is a plethora of men — all tall, muscular, and hunky. There has to be at least fifteen people out there.

Tabitha shakes her head watching me. "Katy will be so upset she missed this. Ridge has done a lot of hiring."

"Katy isn't coming?"

"She doesn't come if it's a couple's thing. She's worried about it. I don't know. I keep telling her it's no big deal, but she doesn't listen."

"Ridge won't let Tabitha anywhere near the grill, so we've been stuck inside keeping the side dishes warm," Winnie says with a laugh and changing the subject.

Tabitha pulls a non-covered casserole dish — what looks to be macaroni and cheese — from the oven and places it on the last bare spot on the counter. "It is for the best," she says, raising one shoulder in a half shrug. I get the impression this is an argument they've before and she's just given up.

"You promise there wasn't a camera in the bathroom?" Anessa asks, walking out from a small powder room off to one side of the kitchen.

A camera?

"He promised the bathrooms and bedrooms are clear," Tabitha says not paying attention as Anessa dries off her hands, whipping them on the top of her jeans.

"Where do you think they are?" Her eyes search the

corners of the room and all the areas where things are gathered.

"Honestly, I've given up trying to figure it out."

Winnie rolls her eyes also checking the spaces with Anessa. "I swear I found one in the bakery. It's tiny, and set into the wall, but it's a camera for sure."

"The cameras aren't that bad. We have used them a few times," Tabitha says, smiling at her friends while their eyes continue to search the room. "I just go with it."

Winnie nods. "You are marrying the man."

Tabitha sighs, one of those deep-gut ones that says she's in love and stares down at her diamond ring. "Yeah."

"Wait a minute," I step toward the girls, still putting all the pieces together. "Ridge has cameras?"

"Everywhere. How do you think he got to the bakery so fast when you guys pulled up with boxes of coke?" Tabitha's eyes widen. She still can't believe we drove a car to Anessa's bakery while it was full of drugs. Neither can I, quite frankly.

"I thought you called them?"

She tips her shoulder up again. "I walked into the back of the bakery and said, 'Hey, Ridge, there's a car of drugs here,' but he already knew. It's the same thing."

Except, it's not. How does she think it's even similar?

"The cameras are nothing, but after the drugs, he brought back the security guard at the bakery. One of his poor guys just sits there all day looking at us."

"The bakery has a security guard?" I ask. I've never seen anyone there.

Anessa nods. "From his company, he and Bennett make somebody sit there all day doing nothing but watching us, eating food, and drinking coffee." She pauses for a moment lost in thought. "Now that I think about it, the guys might not mind the job so much. But it's weird on my end."

"Especially when Dom or one of his brothers comes in." Tabitha uncovers a few more dishes on the counter, balling up tinfoil and throwing it in the trash.

"Who is Dom?"

Anessa leans closer, whispering like she's scared somebody will hear her talking. "He runs the local motorcycle gang. He and Bennett have this uneasy alliance, but I wouldn't call them friendly."

"The alliance or the guys?"

"Bennett and Dom. The actual guys in the club are super nice."

Tabitha nods. "They're at the bakery about once a day and are always polite."

"I don't know why everyone dislikes them," Winnie chips in.

Definitely living in the twilight zone.

The front door opens and a woman's voice calls out. "We're here."

Tabitha comes across the other side of the island and hugs a blonde-haired woman. "Josie this is Joslin. She's dating Spencer. I'm so glad they let him off the cameras for the day so you could eat with us."

"Josie and Jocelyn," Winnie says, staring at the both of us. "What's with all the J names?"

I shrug. "People like J names."

"Anyway," Tabitha says clearing her throat. "We were talking about all the new crazy things the guys are making us do after Katy's little incident with the drugs. What does Spencer have you doing?"

Jocelyn thinks for a second. "I don't have any. He's crazy and protective in general so not much has changed."

Winnie and Tabitha laugh like these conversations are natural.

The back door opens and a tall brown-haired guy peeks his head in. "Hey, Jos. Wanna come hang out with me?"

"She's with the girls," Tabitha yells back, her face perplexed.

The door closes, but Jocelyn's eyes never leave it. "I'll go check on them," she says before hurrying outside.

Winnie shakes her head. "That girl has it bad."

"He has a dog. He roped her in with pet love," Tabitha replies, watching Jocelyn walk across the wooden deck and Spencer wrap his arm around her shoulders before they walk down the steps and into the grass together.

"So what has Nate done to you?" Tabitha asks once the couple is out of sight.

I consider the past few days for a second, trying to go over everything. "Nothing."

But then as a silence sets in and the girls all stare at me waiting, a few things fall into place. Like the fact he has been reluctant to leave me alone the last few days. And on Wednesday when he had to work for a few hours, he had Pearl come over and sit with me. I asked if it was to help with Emma and he nodded but the way he said, "Yeah, Emma," made a few strands of doubt settle deep.

And he put that tracker on my phone.

Although, he did that for my benefit.

Didn't he?

Of course he did. And even if he didn't, the tracker

makes me feel better. But I'm not going to admit it to the room of women looking at me waiting.

"That's what we thought," Winnie says, nodding with understanding, but not asking for more information.

Tabitha pulls the last casserole from the oven, but there's no room left on the island so she forces it on top of the burner. "Even though they're crazy, something about those men keeps us coming back."

I nod, but she doesn't turn around to see.

"Can you help with some of these?" Tabitha asks, already handing us each a pair of oven mitts and grabbing a dish from the counter.

"Sure," I agree sticking my hand in the thick bright pink glove.

Tabitha holds the door open with her butt, letting each of us walk out past her.

I'm halfway down the deck steps when there's a rumble in the air. A motorcycle.

And then another. And then another. And then the sound explodes like it's not one or two guys riding motorcycles together but an entire pack of them. A gang.

10

The noise gets louder and louder until it sounds like the motorcycles stop right on the other side of Ridge's house. I put the casserole down on the wooden picnic table in the middle of the yard, and Nate stands beside me holding Emma to his chest. The fact he's tense doesn't go unnoticed and doesn't make me feel better about the racket happening at the front of the house.

The engines cut off in unison and I hear voices.

From the right corner of Ridge's house walk a large group of men — oversized and wearing more leather than they should in the heat of Pelican Bay summer. They stop at the edge of the yard.

One man in particular with a determined look stands with his arms crossed. His eyes drag through the crowd and stop at Anessa when he nods his head once in her direction. She nods back and then her head tips up, looking at Bennett, who stands by her side with a scowl written across his features.

"I don't remember inviting you," Ridge says, stepping up to the front of his crowd.

From the middle of the yard where Nate and I stand, the scene reminds me of one from *Grease* with the two sides standing off against each other. Except this time one side is nicely dressed in their matching black polo shirts and dark colored jeans and the other with hair slicked back wearing leather and looking as a rugged as possible. I bet at least one of them has a switchblade.

We can only hope it doesn't end the same as in the movie version.

"I don't remember inviting one of your guys to sit outside my shop all week," the clear leader of the pack of motorcyclists says across the yard currently considered as no-man's-land. "You'd think for a security man with such a celebrity status you wouldn't be so obvious."

Ridge laughs but it's forced. "If I didn't want you to know, Dom, you wouldn't. Nate here has so much special-ized training you wouldn't see or hear him coming."

I inch my head back and stare at Nate, silently asking him a hundred questions. Ones he's never answered before. He doesn't this time either. His head tilts down, and he smiles in my direction before giving his attention back to the standoff happening in front of us.

"What I have is some guy named Antonio in Vegas asking me where his storage unit full of drugs is. You know anything about that?"

I freeze. My heart is the only thing moving in my body. Nate wraps his arm around me and hugs me closer, squeezing me a small amount, but it doesn't do enough to release my nerves.

"I don't know. We don't get ourselves mixed up in

those things. Maybe you should hang out with a better circle of friends." Ridge takes one step closer.

It's matched with a step from the other guy, the space between them decreasing with each movement.

"I heard it's not only drugs you're keeping in the *You Store It* outside of town."

The motorcycle boss rolls his eyes, but it doesn't quite match his persona. "And what else has big bad Ridge Jefferson heard?"

"One of the men got a lead on a shipment of guns making their way from Columbia up to Canada. You know how I feel about my town as a shipping point."

The motorcycle leader rears back, surprised by the comment. "I've done my best to turn this club around the last five years, but you still stand over there and accuse me of running guns. Unless it's because you want to have trouble."

Nate steps forward, dropping his hand from my shoulder and passing Emma off to me. I reach out for him but he doesn't grab my hand. Instead he walks all the way up next to Ridge's side. He's followed by a tall guy who leaves Anessa and then another, the name Crispin etched into the pocket of his polo shirt.

"Now, guys," Nate says, putting his hands out toward each man. "You can't expect Ridge not to question the guns if you walk onto his property during a barbecue and accuse him of stealing drugs," Nate says looking at both men. "Everyone has shit in the past they don't want getting out, but the important thing is we've agreed to work together to bring down our mutual threat."

No one else says anything, and the silence grows,

waiting to see where the cards will fall. Nate looks to Ridge. "Right, boss?"

Ridge nods his head but doesn't speak.

"Right, Dom?" Nate asks the leader of the pack standing opposite of him.

The guy in the leather vest with Mother Fucker on it nods too. "We don't want any trouble, but I don't like you bringing it to my backyard either."

"I didn't bring anything here. I'm trying to stop the crews who have run this town for years. If we're going to reclaim it, we have to reclaim it together."

Dom nods again. "That we do, brother."

Nate smiles clapping his hands together. "Perfect, what does everyone want to eat? There's plenty of food for everyone. Right, Tabitha?" Nate asks, searching Tabitha with his eyes and begging her to say yes.

"Of course," she says an easy smile on her face.

That's all it takes before the two men both visibly relax, not to a point they trust each other, but enough that the guys standing behind the motorcycle club leader shuffle in our direction and take up spots at one picnic table the furthest away from the others.

Nate makes his way back to me before I follow Tabitha into the house to get more dishes, and I pull on his arm to get his attention. "What's all that about?"

He smiles. "I'm also a good negotiator. Part of the training."

And that's all he says before he laughs, patting Ridge on the back, and takes Emma over to talk to one of the guys in the motorcycle club with the name Ripper on his chest.

"So, this is what young mothers do on a busy Saturday night?" Nate asks. If he hadn't been chuckling as he questioned my life choices, I would have thought him serious. As it is, the way he smiles and pops another Oreo in his mouth leads me to believe he's not so upset about spending our evening inside.

I lean closer to the side, resting my head on his shoulder. "It's not an exciting life, but someone has to make the sacrifice."

Nate turns, not taking his eyes off the TV and kisses me in the top of my head. "I'll gladly sacrifice with you."

My heart melts. Literally like it just goos out of my chest into a puddle on the ground. What man says the right thing to a woman all the time? And at what point is he going to fade away? I can't stop feeling like my big fairy godmother granted me a wish, but he'll turn back into a pumpkin at midnight.

We've been together pretty much every day and we've fallen into a routine. Breakfast in the morning, seeing Nate off to work, playing with Emma, dinner, and then TV before bed.

I've never cuddled with a man on the couch before now.

It's amazing.

I'm dreading going back to work because my days will get crazier and I'll have less time to see Emma and Nate.

"What are you think about?" Nate asks.

"Nothing," I lie.

He pulls back, separating us a fraction, but I miss his warmth. "You're thinking because she just said she's going to have Italian bricks flown in to complete the patio and you didn't throw a pillow at the television."

My mouth drops open, staring at the TV screen, which has already moved to a commercial. "Italian bricks? What kind of budget does she think they have? It will ruin the project."

"Out with it, Josie. What's bothering you?"

I smile. I've also never had a man concerned with what was bothering me. Everyone has always accepted my "nothing" responses in the past.

"Nothing, I was just thinking of how crappy it will be when I go back to work. I'm gonna miss being home with Emma all day and seeing you."

He squeezes me with the arm wrapped around my back. "Maybe it will work out and you won't have to go back. You never know."

"What does that mean? I like working. I want to keep doing it. I just hate how it interferes with the fun parts of life." My mind fills with vivid images of getting to be a stay-at-home mom to Nate's kids, but that won't happen. I won't allow myself to be into a situation where I don't have to work again. It sounds odd, but getting divorced caught me off guard and I wasn't prepared. I counted on my husband for everything and the day he told me he was leaving, he left me out in the cold with nothing. No job, no savings, and no prospects for the future.

I refuse to let myself fall back into that position ever again, regardless how wonderful the person I'm with treats me at the time.

"What about working part time or something?" His words sound almost hurt as if my response isn't what he expected. I already only work part time.

I do my best to sit up straighter without leaving his side while I share a bit of my past. "When I found out about the cheating with Barry, it was the scariest time of my life. Not because he cheated — although that sucked — but he left me alone with a small child. I had no job and no job prospects. Nowhere to live and no way to pay the bills. It was like I opened my front door one morning and rather than a yard, I saw the black abyss of my future."

I stop talking before the emotions run too high and I cry. Getting angry always made me tear up. The more pissed the more tears.

Nate stares and there's pity in his eyes, which I don't want from him or anyone else. I'm stronger now than ever before and I'm proud of my growth.

"But I'm happy now. I like my job and we have the apartment." At the last minute, I leave out the part where if I don't get back to work soon my savings will end in about four months.

"You'll find this hard to believe, but I understand." He squeezes me once again and then lowers the volume on the TV when it turns back to our show. "My dad and mom divorced when I was ten and until then I'd never seen the woman cry. Every time she checked the mail, one of us heard her in the bedroom crying. There's nothing like being a ten-year-old kid wanting to help your mother and not being able."

"I'm sorry," I say because what else is there?

He snorts, but not over what I've said. "It sucked for a few years, but like you my mother is strong and she came back happier than ever before. If you talk to her now, she would say the divorce was the best thing to ever happen to her."

I nod because I can already see how easily it could be true. Restarting and rebuilding my life with Emma was hard. I hope it's the hardest thing I ever do, but in ways also the best. I wasn't the person I should have been while married, and being on my own has given me the opportunity to find myself. Now, I'm figuring it all out and deciding what I want to be when I grow up, but at least now I have options.

"I just want you to know that I would never do that to you, Josie. You or Emma."

This man. I stare up at Nate, and even though I want to trust him, I can't make myself say the words. They would be a lie. I trusted someone before and look how it ended up for me. "I'm sorry," I whisper. Hopefully he doesn't get mad and storm out.

"It's okay. One day I'll earn your trust and I don't care how long it takes me."

"I hope you do." And I mean it was all my heart. I want to trust Nate, but I worry that part of me is broken forever.

He turns back to the television, but it's a commercial again. "Do you know why I came to work for Ridge?"

I think for a moment. "Because you heard Pelican Bay was a hopping town to live in and you couldn't wait to meet me?"

He laughs. "Yes, all those reasons, but also because when Ridge talked to me about joining his team, one thing he said stuck out. They were a family. As a child, my family was very close after my dad left. We only had each other and then each of my siblings got married and had kids and I joined the military where I met a new family. In what felt like a heartbeat, it was time for my service to end and I faced my dark future. Nowhere near as scary as yours, but for the first time in my life I had to go out into the world alone without a family."

I nod because I understand how that could be scary and terrifying. Even for a big tough SEAL.

"Ridge talked about the group of men he wanted to put together and how he considered us a family. At that point I didn't care how much the pay was or what I had to do. I just wanted to be here and get a new family. Find my people again."

"And you like them?"

"Ridge and the guys are great, and even though Pelican Bay is smaller than what I thought, I like the town. And the people."

"We are interesting people. Aren't we?" I took this apartment because it was cheapest and available, but I always planned to move closer to Clearwater where I work. However, after experiencing Pelican Bay, I changed my plans, deciding instead to look for something by the ocean.

"There's one thing I didn't plan for when I moved here. For the first time in my life, being surrounded by a group of SEALS isn't enough family. I'd like to start my own."

My stomach clenches in anticipation of what his words mean. Is it wrong of me to get so excited about a new relationship after my divorce? I told myself no more dating because men only caused problems, but I'd consider tossing it out the window for Nate. Could a man as nice, caring, and cute as Nate want to start a family with someone like me who already has a daughter and an ex-husband? He could find a beautiful, no baggage woman.

"Don't freak out. I'm not asking you to marry me," he says with a smile. "Although the way your body is tense right now, I'm a little worried if I ever popped the question."

I laugh, trying to cover up my fears, and push against his chest. "We haven't been together long enough to have the family talk." Even though I wish we could. If only Nate and I had met before I had a past knocking at my back door.

"It is too soon. I'm not making any promises right now, but I want you to know where I'm coming from. Josie, I'm not looking for a two-month stand. I promise I wouldn't be in Emma's life if I didn't plan to be here a while, and I want to be in both your lives for as long as possible."

Hearing him say he wants to be in our lives creates another little crack in the wall formed in my chest keeping me from trusting. It's too soon.

Neither of us are ready to say the words yet, but I hope he has found a family in Emma and me. I never thought I could be taken with a person — especially after the divorce — but as corny as it sounds Nate and I have a connection. Being with him doesn't make me feel like I have to fill every second with mindless chatter. I don't have to dress up and look perfect every time he's in the room. With him I can be myself. It's as if before I met him, I was running around looking for the second half of my soul. Now that Nate is here, I've been stitched back together. It's a weird feeling I can't escape even though my brain isn't ready to accept I'm ready to love again. The L-word was supposed to be far away in my distant future, not staring at me in the face while sitting on my couch.

But the emotions become too much and the topic too heavy. The room fills with the silence between us as I process what he said. It's too much for me to handle right now, so rather than jump into his lap and tell him yes please take me away, I laugh pretending the moment is lighthearted even though it isn't. At least not for me.

"I have so much family that if you stick around, you'll regret those words. The only thing my mother loves more than hating people is helping make them better."

Nate laughs, sticking to my ploy of lightening the mood. "What you're saying is I can expect to wear a lot of khakis in my future?"

I start to say yes but stop myself. "No, I want you to be who you are." No one should have to change for my mother, and for the first time in my life, I don't care if she likes Nate or not. I like him and that's good enough for me. I'm the one who has to live with the choices I make, so I'm the only one who gets a say in them from now on.

NATE GIVES Emma a kiss on the cheek, making sure it's extra slobbery, and then passes her off to me.

"Do you think she likes vanilla or chocolate?" Tabitha asks from behind the bakery counter.

Nate's head lifts up, looking at the two cupcakes Tabitha holds out, one in each hand. "Chocolate, of course."

"Nate, are you sure we want to pump her full of

sugar?" I ask tentatively. Sure, she's getting older and has had sugar before, but Emma has enough energy on her own. I can't imagine what she'll be like on a full cupcake.

When he mentioned bringing Emma to the bakery so I could talk with the girls while he went to work for a few hours, he never said anything about letting her consume large amounts of chocolate. The cupcake is half the size of her head. Chocolate and Emma aren't always such the good mix. There's no telling how it will go.

"She loves chocolate," Nate says in a singsong voice, getting close to Emma's face. "Doesn't my little girl love chocolate?"

She hits him on the nose, and from the way he leans back smiling, I'm pretty sure he takes it as a yes.

"I wish I had a highchair for the bakery," Anessa says walking over to the counter and handing Nate the chocolate cupcake. "It's the first thing I'll add to my next shopping list. I'm sorry,"

Nate takes the cupcake from her, using his finger to wipe off a small piece of the chocolate frosting and letting Emma stuck it off his finger. When I was a new mother, I would've been disgusted because who knows where his finger has been. But now I don't know what the hell she's eating half the time. Probably 75 percent of the food that makes it in her mouth touched the floor first. I have bigger priorities, like making sure she doesn't run off and get lost. At some point we must get this potty-training thing started, too.

"If I leave, do you promise to stay in the building?" Nate asks, looking me in the eyes.

My word, make one little run to your storage unit and

then drive through town with a car full of drugs and everyone acts like you need a babysitter.

I widen my eyes so he can see how honest my answer is. "Nate, I promise. I would never do anything with Emma." What kind of parent does he think I am? Yes, I might let her listen Eminem but I wouldn't risk her life.

"Nate, go do what you have to do. She'll be fine here. If anything happens, we have our own undercover special agent right here with Crispin." Anessa points out the same man I saw step up with Nate and Ridge during the confrontation with the motorcycles.

The blond-haired, dark-eyed man lowers the book he's been reading — making me think he wasn't reading all — and gives Anessa a look. Then with a fingertip to his lips he shakes his head at her. "Shhhs."

Anessa rolls her eyes from behind the counter but Crispin only smiles.

"How long are you on crap duty, Crispin?" Nate asks.

Tabitha scoffs. "We're not crap duty."

"Regardless, Tabitha's right," Anessa butts in. "We are *the* Bakery Bandit girls and being stationed in the bakery is a high honor. Plus I pump them full of chocolate and food all day."

Crispin smiles. "It's a hard job, but somebody has to do it until *You Know Who* gets taken care of," he says looking at Nate.

Nate nods as if he knows who he's discussing. I have a feeling I do too.

"Make sure and keep your eye on Josie, Crispin" Nate says leaning down and giving Emma a quick kiss on top of her head and then me a matching one.

"Take care of my girls and make sure she gets all the cupcakes she wants."

"You'll change her diapers tonight," I yell, as he walks out the door.

Nate holds the door open for Pearl as she walks into the bakery, and she turns back, spending a few seconds watching him leave. "That man. I don't know how you are so lucky to end up with the backside that dude is sporting."

The word dude coming from the older woman's mouth is weird and off-putting, but then so are half the things Pearl says.

She sits down at her favorite table and Crispin raises his book, pretending to read again.

"Although if you had seen Roland in his younger days. Tsk tsk tsk. That man was a looker. We used to get it on three times a day."

"Pearl!" Tabitha says.

Crispin lifts his book a little higher, and I swear his ear turns a shade of red.

Pearl rolls her eyes. "Don't tell me you aren't, ladies. If you aren't, then you are not using your time effectively. You're young right now. Don't waste these years of flexibility."

Anessa wipes her hands on her pink apron and brings over a teacup of water and tea bag for Pearl, setting them on her plate.

"Why don't you set Emma down with me so she can eat that cupcake she's staring at like it's life's answer to living." Pearl pats the seat on the other side of her small round table.

I consider it for a second, but then I visualize Emma

falling off the chair when she falls into a sugar coma and can't sit still.

"Make the tough guy hold her," Pearl says, using her thumb to point back at Crispin.

"Me?" he asks with a smidge of fear.

My eyes light up at the idea. He'd never let anything happen to Emma because Nate would have a fit. "Would you? Please?"

He sighs, resigned to his fate, and closes his book without even bothering to use a bookmark. Then he gets up and moves to the other side of Pearl's table. I place Emma in his lap and the cupcake on the table and try to turn the other direction so I don't witness the horror that's about to happen. I'm not sure this is part of the job these tough guys signed up for when Ridge recruited them.

"Nate sure has taken to her. Hasn't he?" Pearl asks, dropping her tea bag in the cup of water.

The kisses, baby talk, and the way he talks about Emma. The way she reaches for him when she cries, knowing Nate will give in to whatever her demands are at the time. All the memories bring a smile to my face as I think about how, yes, Nate *has* taken to her. And she to him.

"He's been great." And I think if he was doing it for my sake he would've cracked by now. He wouldn't have gotten up with her multiple times in the middle of night when she was sick.

"What about her father? Is he in her life? Will that become an issue?" Pearl asks.

Tabitha shakes her head, going back behind the

counter. "Pearl is not one to mince words," she whispers before leaving me to the wolf.

"He sees her once a month, sometimes twice. Barry is a very busy with his new girlfriend. When we first split up, he saw her often but now that I've moved further away and his girlfriend becomes more demanding, he's seeing her less and less." Each visit he drops her off a little earlier on Sunday afternoon.

"I hate men like that," Anessa says, pulling a knife high in the air. "I want to walk up and tell every single one of them off." She stabs at the cake, sliding the knife all the way through to cut a piece for Pearl in one fluid motion. Remind me to never upset that woman.

"I can see that." Tabitha removes the knife from Anessa's hands, allowing her to put the piece of cake on a plate and walk it to Pearl. "No one give her sharp knives when she's worked up."

"Well, it is ridiculous. You meet a guy and give him so much of your life and what does he do?"

"Throws it away for bitches and drugs," Tabitha hollers and then shrugs and we all look in her direction. "Hey, it happens. Happened to me."

"Exactly who is your ex?" I ask Tabitha. She's never given me the whole story.

She pinches her face together like she doesn't want to tell me. "He was a lot of things, but I didn't see him for any of them until I left and then the truth came out."

I nod, understanding what she's saying. I thought I was married to a completely honest man, yet the longer we were apart after the divorce the truth of who my husband was slowly seeped to the surface. Why couldn't I see it before?

"Well you let us know if he causes any trouble because we've got your back," Anessa says, pointing between her and Tabitha, who hides the knife in the small sink behind the counter.

Emma squeals, drawing my attention, and I look over to find her face covered in chocolate. You can't even see her nose holes she has so much shoved up them. It's like I put the cupcake down on the table and she smashed her face into it trying to get as much chocolate in her mouth as quickly as possible. Crispin searches me with his eyes in a pleading look as he holds Emma on his lap while trying his best not to touch any of her parts covered in sticky chocolate.

Emma flails her hands wildly, and she hits him in the chin, splattering frosting all over his jaw. Crispin's mouth falls open in disgust and he closes his eyes.

"I hope Spencer can take still shots in the video feed because we need this moment to live on forever," Tabitha says not taking her eyes off Crispin. "Did you hear that, Spencer?" she questions, loudly at the camera she must believe is in the corner of the room. "Still shots!"

"So sorry." I go to his side and relieve him of Emma so he can go to the bathroom and clean up. Emma doesn't care at all. She squishes the cupcake with her hand and squeals, smashing a few last bites in her mouth. The door to the bakery opens, and a customer walks in as I work to clean up the crumbles of chocolate cupcake surrounding Emma on the floor. No one seems to mind or bother she's made a huge mess. For just a second, during the brief period Emma lets me sit peacefully, my eyes circle the bakery and I breathe a sigh of relief. I may have been searching most of my life, but the time has finally come. I found where I belong.

A BIT OF WIND — a cool blast off the ocean's waves — twists my hair and pushes past where Nate, Emma, and I walk along the beach. Emma squeals in her stroller. She's always loved to be near the water.

"Are you cold?" Nate asks, looking at the goosebumps running across my arms.

I wipe them away and they stay gone. "No, every once in a while the breeze picks up, but I'm not ready to go back."

We spent the day together, walking the beach hand in hand. Emma played in the sand, knocking down all the tall sand castles Nate worked so desperately hard to build for her. It was a wonderful afternoon. The sun warmed my skin, and the birds squawked in the sky while the waves crashed against the shore. It has been one of those days I'll remember for the rest of my life but each time I'll wonder if it was as amazing as I recall. It'll seem too good to be true.

But that's what it is. Perfect.

Nate stops and then pushes down the parking brake on the stroller. He stares out into the water with his attention slowly working its way down the sky and stares at the waves as they crash on the shore.

"I wasn't sure what I expected to find what I moved here, but it's gorgeous."

Together we stare out at the view and I nod standing next to him. I've lived near the water most my life, but there's something special about the way the bay comes in and the land forms around the sea at large. Pelican Bay has its own special ocean, just for the lucky people who know of this place.

"So many people think of beautiful sunsets on the water happening in the South like Florida or California, but it's just gorgeous up here." Maine is so misunderstood.

"I thought this was something you only see in Florida."

Wait until Nate sees his first whale. It may not be as warm in this part of northern Maine but it's beautiful.

"I can see myself spending the rest of my life here," he says, and it's so nonchalant he doesn't notice how his words affect me.

But they do. Was there a point in time he hadn't planned to live here forever? "Do you plan to leave?" I ask, trying my best not to be shaken by fear.

"No, not now," he says, not taking his eyes from the view. "When I first moved, I wasn't so sure I'd make it. I'm used to the big city and Pelican Bay is far from city life."

I laugh. Most of Maine is far from city life. "Was growing up in LA fun?" I've never been, but being surrounded by celebrities seems like it could have its perks.

Contrary to what I expect, Nate shakes his head. "A lot of smog, cars, and homeless. People think of Hollywood and the celebrities, but there's many more people who are barely making it than those who live in mansions."

There's an income difference here as well. Not everyone lives in large mansions like Pierce Kensington.

Most people have medium to even small-sized homes packed together in the downtown area. And even those cost a fortune. If you polled the people of Pelican Bay, most wouldn't even say they wanted the big mansion but preferred a little cabin in the woods surrounded by nature. Life is simpler here and in most people's opinions a lot better that way. I agree with them.

"Maybe for Christmas I'll go home and visit my family," he says and then his eyes fall to Emma. "If you're allowed to go?"

The question isn't direct, but I understand what he's asking. We've had this discussion before about who gets Emma on holidays. Barry doesn't care for most of them, but Christmas is one he makes me alternate.

"I'll check the calendar and see if this year is my turn have Emma for Christmas." I hate the idea of having to spend a holiday without her. A part of me hopes my ex will stop caring and let me keep her every year, but that makes me a bad mother. Her father should be in her life even if I hate him.

"Either way we'll make sure Emma has a great Christmas."

My breath stalls and then picks up quickly. Nate may not realize what he's said, but I do. My heart and brain both jump in glee. He is thinking about what we'll be doing this holiday season — which is months away, an entire summer and fall. I haven't even thought about Christmas yet. I'm still trying to survive this month.

Nate checks his watch and then unlocks the stroller and walks down the sidewalk, which separates the public beach from the rest of Pelican Bay.

"Do you want to stop and get some ice cream?" he

asks as we get closer to the ice-cream stand.

A small rectangular building sits in the middle of the parking lot connected to the beach. I've tried to say away because my hips don't need the calories, but they have the best soft serve I've ever eaten. Besides, I'm pretty sure they're putting something else besides milk and sugar in it.

"I think she's out," I say, leaning forward to look in the stroller and see a sleeping child. Emma hasn't made a noise for the last five minutes, which is a dead giveaway that at some point her eyes rolled back and she passed out. It doesn't happen often, but occasionally she falls asleep the same way she wakes up in the morning zero to sixty.

Nate laughs. "It's for the best. I will have nightmares for months about that diaper you made me change. Who knew that color could come from a baby?"

"I tried to warn you. Chocolate does something to Emma."

"You know what?" Nate asks, looking off into the distance across the street from where we stand. "You deserve an adult dessert."

"An adult dessert?"

Nate looks back, his eyes narrowed my direction, and then his lips tip up into a smile. "Not that kind of dessert. Something with cake in it." He pauses, checking for traffic as we cross the road. "But if you want to get kinky with cake, I'd be up for it."

"Kinky with cake?" A blush stains my cheeks, thinking about what that could mean. I may never walk into the bakery without getting some kind of bedroom cake image in my head again.

11

Nate walks us right up to the Pelican Bay Bed and Breakfast, using the ramp to get Emma past all the steps. The hostess meets us at the door and he asks to be seated on the patio.

"Wow, I can't believe they have an opening," I whisper as the blonde-haired hostess leads us to one of the large open patios facing the water. In the past, I've tried to eat here before when my mother was in town, but reservations happen weeks in advance over the summer.

Nate checks his watch. "Not many people coming in for dinner at 9 p.m."

He has a point.

The waitress steps up to our table as soon as the hostess steps away. A few pieces of hair have slipped from her bun and her eyes are droopy.

"Hi, my name is Sammie and I'll be your waitress tonight. The kitchen is closing down and shutting off ovens, but we offer cold items from the fridge. Salads and chilled pastas."

"That's okay, Sammie. We're just here for dessert. Can we have those menus?" Nate asks, handing back the dinner menu she passed his way. He readjusts Emma's stroller between us and covers her with the extra blanket shoved in the side as he smiles down at her sleeping form. Those little gestures show so much.

Sammie sighs with relief. "Of course. I'll bring out the cart."

"A cart?" I haven't eaten at a restaurant with a cart for desserts since I was married.

Nate doesn't have time to answer before Samantha sweeps back with the cart pushed in front of her. She's walking ten miles an hour, her legs pumping to quicken her pace. Fake desserts highlight what they offer on the cart for patrons to look at and make a selection.

It takes less than a nano second for me to decide what I want. "Do you have that big chocolate thing in a smaller size?"

Not that I couldn't eat the entire Molten Lava cake by myself, but I'd rather not when Nate's around.

He laughs. "Get a full one and I'll eat half. If you're okay with that?" he questions, looking up into my eyes. Like I would ever say no.

I nod. I'm okay sharing dessert with Nate forever.

"You're sure it's okay?" Nate asks again once the waitress leaves.

I hold back a laugh. "Do I look that hungry? Of course. I couldn't eat the whole thing myself." Lies.

"Look at that sunset," Nate says, turning his chair a bit to get a better view of the ocean from our spot on the patio and completely changing the subject. His hair blows in the breeze coming off the water and his smile glows in the lights from the ocean.

I turn, following his direction, and am taken aback by the pink hues that flood the sky. They turn each cloud into its own painted canvas. Sunsets in Maine don't happen over the water — the whole East coast thing — but it doesn't mean you don't get a gorgeous feel on the opposite side. If you want to see the full beauty, you've got to get up in the morning.

"I hope I get to see a million more of these with you, Josie." Nate glances across the table smiling sweetly.

I look down, not sure to how respond, but take his hand when he reaches for mine. "Me too." We're moving so fast, something I never expected to happen, but I'm full of feelings I didn't believe I'd experience. There's no way to turn off what I feel or slow down our relationship. I'm no longer driving the bus.

The sun falls further in the sky behind us and I breathe in the ocean air, letting it relax me as I work to remember every piece of this moment.

Samantha clears her throat and I'm jostled back to reality as our waitress sets down the dessert plate on the table between us. "If you need anything else, please let me know," she says, also placing down two waters that we didn't order but I'm glad she brought.

THE YOKE of one of my eggs pops, the gooey yellow substance running over and sizzling in the pan.

Screw it.

Breakfast just became scrambled eggs.

Emma squeals in the living room as Nate chases her around wielding a hairbrush like a sword and I chop up the egg into pieces pretending like they were scrambled all along.

The toaster pops, and before I can turn around to grab the warm bread to slather it in butter, Nate is there taking out the four pieces.

"I got it," he says, grabbing a butter knife from the drawer.

"Did you talk Emma out of wearing the dress?" I ask. They don't care if she wears dresses at daycare but want them to have shorts on underneath. It sounded like a simple enough request, but Emma hates wearing shorts — a fact I didn't learn until recently when she kept pulling them off halfway through the day and her daycare kept sending me texts about it. Like I could somehow make her keep them on from my desk in Clearwater.

He nods and cuts a piece of toast in half before sprinkling pepper over a small portion of the eggs off to one side.

"Hey! Emma can't have pepper."

"Just separate them," he says bumping me with his hip and stealing my position in front of the stove, which forces me to step to the side. "We'll cook this half away from her half." He uses the spatula to divide the two eggs, slipping the peppered eggs to the side of the pan.

Nate is cute, good with the baby, and he cooks. How did I win the man lottery?

At times like this, I wonder if he hit me with his truck a little harder than I realized and I'm in a coma in the hospital and this is all a dream. One day I'll wake up and five years will have gone by where I lay in the hospital bed dreaming up the perfect man.

Nate isn't distracted daydreaming in the middle of the kitchen. He grabs two juice glasses and set them on the counter before filling each up with orange juice.

"Here I'll take them to the table," I say, trying to be a little helpful.

I give Emma a small plate of eggs and she claps her hands twice, smiling. We both know where these eggs are going, and for most of them it won't be her mouth. She's wearing a black pair of leggings and an oversized purple shirt with Disney's little mermaid screen-printed on the front. Something isn't right, and it takes me a moment to put my finger on what's off. Nate's new ability to coordinate the outfit doesn't catch me off my guard. It's the fact Emma's hair looks...

Normal.

Two little pigtails, both containing almost the same amount of hair, stick out evenly from the sides of her head.

"Did you do Emma's hair?" I ask thinking maybe in my morning frazzlesness I forgot I put them in this morning.

Nate stops by the table with one hand on his hip admiring his work. "I did. Only took six tries, but look at how even they are."

I nod. Six tries isn't that bad. Some days it's taken me more, especially if she's feeling wiggly.

"You did great, Nate." I tap the knuckle of my index finger on the table before sitting down to eat breakfast.

Then sitting at the table with Nate across from me and Emma to my side, each of us eating our own plate of eggs, it hits me. It's a Monday morning. It's my first day back to work, which means Nate is also going to work and Emma will go back into daycare.

It's a day I've lived many times before. Well, never with Nate here, but breakfast with Emma before daycare is a scene I should be used to at this point.

But for some reason I don't want to send my rambunctious toddler back to a daycare center with thirty-five other children. I want to be at home with her. It's quiet as we eat, no one noticing the life-changing freak-out happening in my brain. Everything I've said and believed since the divorce doesn't sound as sane as it did days ago.

I meant it when I told Nate I never want to find myself in the same position Barry left me in with the divorce. At first the job search had been so stressful I didn't think I'd make it, but I enjoy working. Bank accounts in my name and making my own decisions helped me gain confidence. The last year was hard, but also satisfying. Would it be so horrible if I found another person, a man like Nate, to put my trust in at some point? Could I love that way again?

I thought I had my life all planned out, but fate had a different plan for me. Barry might have been an ass, but his actions didn't reflect on me. I wish I had caught him cheating sooner, but there's nothing to be done about it now.

Even going to work this morning I'm happier now than when I was married. I've smiled more and enjoyed life more with Nate and Emma these last few weeks than in the last few years.

Nate's hand flies into the air and he catches the first

bit of eggs before they hit the wall. Emma laughs, but from the look on her face she doesn't plan to give up on her mission to redecorate anytime soon.

He gets her to eat a forkful of egg pretending it's an airplane — I don't understand how the trick works on her — and she happily chews them as he smiles with pride.

It is almost too perfect. I worry what will happen if I enjoy myself too much. Will God come and take something away? Seems to happen with my life. If I get too happy, the barrel of my good luck will tip over and spill out.

"What are you doing at work today?" I ask, forgetting Nate doesn't have a normal job in my quest to move on from the sobering topic happening in my brain. "Never mind," I finish when I remember he can't tell me.

He laughs. "Today I will be manning the cameras in the office."

My eyes widened. "Really? No secret spy business today?"

He shakes his head. "Although, some days interesting things go down on cameras." The way he says it has me narrow in my eyes as if I stare at him long enough maybe I can see what he means. I suspect it has to do with the tiny incident involving the storage unit visit. Or Emma's adventure with chocolate.

"Why are you on camera duty?" I don't know what Nate normally does, but it seems like a downgrade going from spying on the motorcycle club to watching a bunch of cameras for a day. How many cameras could there be for him to watch?

He shrugs. "Spencer's dog ate some carpet and needs surgery."

"Carpet?"

Nate shakes his head. "Not the weirdest thing the dog has ingested, believe it or not, but I guess this time it was like half the living room or something."

"This time?" Pictures of a living room with half the carpet missing and a trail hanging from the dog's mouth make me reconsider getting pets. Maybe I just became a fish person.

"Oh shit." I say checking my watch. "I'm going to be late."

My eyes fall to Emma as I calculate how long it will take me to get her all the way to daycare and then get back to the office in Clearwater. I haven't made the drive lately and have forgotten how far it is. There isn't much traffic in this area, but when there is, it's a bitch.

"Hurry, Emma, we've got to go."

Nate grabs my plate and empty glass of orange juice after I finished sucking down the last gulp and takes them to the kitchen. "I can take Emma to daycare. It's practically on the way."

Her daycare is only a mile down the road, but with morning traffic it takes at least fifteen minutes to do a drop off. Especially if I talk to any of the workers. If I let Nate do it, it would cut out a serious portion of my morning drive.

I reluctantly disagree. Emma is my responsibility, and I can't pass her off on him whenever I need a little help, but Nate's not having any of it.

"If you don't want me to, I won't. I was just trying to be nice and help you out."

I stare into his deep eyes and laugh at myself for being selfish. "It's not that I don't trust you or anything. I just want to say goodbye to on her first day back to daycare, but it's fine."

Satisfied with my answer, he grabs Emma from her high chair and I give her three more kisses as I buckle her into the car seat in the back of my car. I won't let Nate drive her in his pickup truck, so he asked to drive my car. I'm sure the guys at his office will give him crap, but the fact he's willing to sit in my tiny little car means the world.

Without my boot — I haven't worn it in the last two days — I'm ready to go back to work. I'll miss Emma and Nate, but I'm ready to get back to my outside life and contribute to the world.

Nate and Emma turn one direction out of the parking lot and I go the opposite way. Without them in Nate's truck, I can turn the radio station up as loudly as I want, and I like my music loud. The windows shake as I drive the twenty minutes to work. My office is in the center of Clearwater, and while it's a small town, it does have two stop lights and a four-way blinking light. More than Pelican Bay has even considered.

I make sure and turn the music down before I pull into the parking lot. I wouldn't want anyone in my job to realize I like my music a little sweary. The door to the community offices is open as I step inside putting my mostly empty briefcase over my shoulder. My ankle, without the protective boot or crutches, makes jumping from the truck an adventure, but I manage without falling on my ass.

It isn't until I hit the sidewalk that my nerves spike.

I've missed weeks of work and have no idea what is waiting for me inside, probably a mound of paperwork. I should have checked in more, but the few emails I tried to send to my boss were all met with reminders that working while out on a sick leave was against the rules.

Regardless of how much paperwork awaits me, I'm ready to get back to work and have a little normality in my life.

Except there's a problem because when I get to my desk at the far back room in the hallway, someone else is sitting there. She's cute, short blonde hair with the brightest blue eyes. She looks up at me and I can tell the moment she figures out who I am because her body freezes and she hesitates before growing fearful like she's a turtle about to climb into her shell and hide.

"You're Josie," she says, her voice shaking.

I nod. "And who are you?"

Her eyes fall to an area next to the desk and mine travel with them. On the floor in one corner there's a box with a few possessions in it. My possessions. The picture of Emma and me at our first day in Pelican Bay we stopped by the beach to count the seagulls. And the frame of finger painting she made during her first week of daycare. My items, possessions, things I brought to this job are tucked away in a box beside the desk.

What the hell?

"Um...." She plays with her hair, not making eye contact. "I think you should talk to Janet."

Janet? My boss. An inkling of what's happening here settles in and I get cranky. "Fine, I'll do that."

Did they hire someone new and there weren't any other offices they could stick her in? Where am I going to work? Why didn't someone mention this in one of the many emails I sent that they barely responded to over the last few weeks?

Janet's office is three doors down and I don't bother knocking when I turn the handle and let myself in. Her eyes widen when she sees me and she gets off her phone call.

"Josie, we didn't expect you today. Why don't you sit down?" she says, motioning to the chair in front of her desk.

I do, but only because I don't want to seem rude by turning down the invitation.

"What's going on here, Janet?" They actually *were* expecting me today. I told them in my last e-mail.

To her credit she looks upset for a moment before she begins talking. "Josie, when you didn't know when you were coming back, we had to hire someone to do your job and she's worked out well."

"Okay and..." I don't finish my sentence waiting for her to do it.

"We've decided we're going to keep Stephanie and let you go. It's nothing personal. You did a great job, but Stephanie doesn't have the same time constraints."

I hesitate for a second letting my brain works through what she said. "You're letting me go? But I had a doctor's note."

Janet nods her head. "Yes, but you didn't work here long enough for that to mean anything. You're still in the six-month probationary period and you missed weeks of work. We had to do something. Stephanie is the mayor's niece, and she jumped right into the opening. I hope you understand."

I most certainly do not. This was my job. *My* job.

My eyes blink rapidly as I sit in the chair unmoving. I understand what she's saying, but I don't understand it either. What will I do now? How will I provide for Emma? Where will we live?

I swallow hard, refusing to cry in front of her. I don't care if I end up living back in my mother's house listening to her tell me "I told you so" every day for the rest of my life. I refuse to let anyone else see me cry.

Without another word to Janet, I nod my head and stand. Screw her.

"If you need a reference, Josie, you know I'll give you a good one," she yells after me as I walk out of her doorway, nodding like I'm okay with everything that has gone down in the last hour.

I stop in my old office and grab my box of stuff, not talking to Stephanie, who doesn't give me the same reassurances of a good reference. Screw her too.

The walk to my car and drive back to Pelican Bay happen in silence, and when I get to my apartment building, I keep driving. I'm not sure where I'm headed, but I know I can't go back and sit in an empty living room today. I need something to help get me through.

Something chocolate.

12

Chocolate and Nate would be best, but I can't bother him while he's at work. I refuse to be that helpless in my life. The money I received in the divorce, which I planned to supplement my income for the next sixteen years while Emma is living at home, has dwindled down to nearly nothing. Before I realized it, needing a job became a serious concern. Expenses kept piling up when I wasn't looking.

I drive down Main Street in Pelican Bay, intending to head to the beach and clear my thoughts by listening to the waves crash against the shore, but the smell of fresh baked bread forces my car to pull over into a space in front of the bakery.

I walk in the front doors not talking to anyone, but Anessa takes one look at me and pulls a chocolate cupcake from her display case. The frosting is white with black specks and it's easy to figure out the flavor with the circular Oreo placed on top standing straight up in the frosting.

"You look like you need this," she says, handing me the cupcake.

I take it without complaint and sit down on the opposite side of the little table that usually houses Pearl. "Thanks." I take off the Oreo and nibble at the sides, hoping I can make the chocolate last as long as I need it.

A lifetime.

My phone rings, and even though I don't want to, I reach into my bag I brought in with me and pull it out. Nate's name is on the screen and I answer. Hopefully, hearing his voice will help.

"Josie, what's wrong," he asks, frantically. "Is everything okay with Emma?"

I hesitate before answering. "What do you mean what's wrong?"

"You look distraught. Do you need help?" Nate says into the phone.

"How do you know what I look like?" I ask, and Anessa looks at me smiling, her eyes moving to the corner of the room.

It's quiet on the line for a moment and then he speaks. "Because the bakery is lined with cameras. You know this. I'm on camera duty today."

"You're watching *those* cameras?" When he said he was on cameras, I thought he'd be watching people's homes or something, not the bakery. Ridge has somebody watching the bakery at all times? That's weird as hell. I thought they were being sarcastic or dramatic. I try to think back to all the things I've done while in the bakery but can't remember anything I've done to make a fool of myself that one of them might relay back to him.

What if they keep copies of stupid stuff like one of those video-clip shows?

"Do you guys save these videos?" Are there any of me? Do you get together with a bucket of popcorn and re-watch them for fun on Friday nights?

"That's unimportant, babe. Tell me what's wrong." He doesn't say no to reassure me they aren't saved.

"I lost my job," I choke out as quietly as possible, fearful if I say anything more I will cry.

Nate sighs on the other end. "That sucks, babe. But it'll be okay."

"I don't see how it will be okay. How will I make rent this month, or next, or the one after? Or buy food?"

Anessa's eyes widen behind the counter and she brings me out another cupcake, placing it next to the one I'd set down to answer the phone.

"I'll take care of you," Nate says.

But what he doesn't understand is I don't want a man to care for me. It sounds nice, but I want to make my own money, buy my own stuff, and be a grown up. Why is that a bad thing?

"I liked that job," I lie. Janet always had that look on her face. The one that said to watch your back, but it was good pay for part-time hours.

"Listen, Josie, I understand you're upset, but don't worry. We'll figure it out. Okay?" Nate sounds so sure of himself and promising that I nod even though I can't see it. There is no easy fix to this.

I breathe deeply once, trying to calm myself and think of the Oreos, and then agree before we say quick goodbyes.

"You know what we should have done?" Katy asks,

popping up from the bottom of the bakery counter where I didn't even see her before. "Saved one of those boxes of drugs. We could have sold it on the side and made a killing."

"Katy!" Anessa says, shaking her head at her friend.

It's not the advice I want or need to hear, but it brings a smile to my face. I don't know Katy well, but I know her enough that I should question whether she's serious. I can't imagine the medium height woman selling drugs, even if it meant paying the bills. But if anyone would, my money is on Katy.

"What? It's the truth and if Pierce raises the rent anymore, we'll all have to get into the drug trade to pay the bills."

Anessa shakes her head. "Did Pierce raise the rent?"

Katy narrows her eyes at her. "No, but he threatens."

"So sorry about the job, Josie," Winnie says, not giving Katy any extra attention.

I take a bite out of the cupcake and sit quietly chewing for a moment. "Ugh... I don't know what I'll do. Nate says don't worry about it, we'll figured out, but I don't know how."

Winnie nods like she understands. "If I were you, I'd let the big guy handle it. Life always works out somehow."

"I can't let Nate help me out when we've just met and started dating." I'm already asking him for so much. I can't add more. My luggage cart is full. Any more baggage will topple it over.

Winnie laughs. "He'll enjoy getting to save the day."

"Oh."

Annessa sighs. "I argued with Bennett for so long

about whether I could handle it on my own, and it was stupid. I wish I would have let him take care of things in the beginning. Sometimes we need help in life and it doesn't make it less or anything."

Katy looks at her dreamily, nodding her head. "If I had a man offer to pay for all my bills, you can bet I would take him up on it. Whatever his credit card could handle."

"I fell for Bennett so hard and fast. I swear it happened the first time I met him. It was fate."

I pull off the bottom of my cupcake and shove it in my mouth, staring at the woman. "He hit me with his truck." Was that fate?

"From what I hear, Huxley almost hit Winnie with his truck. And look at them."

"Don't give the men any more ideas. Next thing you know they'll be knocking women over with vehicles all over Pelican Bay," Katy says, rearranging a few trays of cookies and bagels in the top row of the rack.

"Fate is fate."

"Not when it's vehicular manslaughter," Katy says, wiping her eyes.

Anessa shakes her head. "Katy, how can you be such a romantic and such a cynic?

"It's easy. First, I remember what I want my life to be and then I realize what life is actually like," Katy replies.

The two women go back to squabbling back and forth over whether Katy needs a man in her life and I study my cupcake, hoping Nate's cameras can't see into my brain to figure out what I'm thinking. It would be so easy to let him take care of things, and I've had a few moments where that was my entire plan, but letting go is a lot harder than people realize. Being the damsel in distress looks better on paper than in real life.

I just came out of a relationship where I trusted the man with everything and he left me for another woman, literally out in the cold. There's no way I can allow that to happen again for me or Emma's sake. I'd love to believe Nate is the one for me, but I'm not sure if I've gotten better at reading people. I certainly haven't done such a good job in the past.

But I want to be because a lot of what Anessa says rings true. I've fallen for Nate hard. Like way hard. He could be *the one* I see myself spending the rest of my life waking up next to every single morning. I promised the next time I dated someone I would take it slowly, but everything with him happened so fast. Nate is everything I dreamed about having in a man when I was married, and I want to stick him into our family like superglue and make sure he can never get away.

AFTER A QUICK CAR switch at the Pelican Bay Security office where I managed to swap cars with Nate before he saw me, I picked up Emma at daycare. Wanting to get us home for the night so I could continue on with my pity-fest. Emma's car seat buckle is difficult, and today is no different as I work to jab the metal into the bottom connector. The five-point harness might be safer for children, but does a number on parents' nerves.

"We're going home to get some dinner," I say to Emma, trying to maintain an upbeat personality. I faked it for the last few hours, sitting at the bakery and listening to the general chatter of bakery customers. The time to go came upon me quickly. I needed to leave, pick up Emma, and come home to face the fact that tomorrow I didn't have a job to go to anymore.

And Emma doesn't have a daycare provider. They weren't too happy when I explained I needed a few more weeks of time off until I found a new job. There are four more days left on our contact and then I'm sure when I find a new job, I'll need to locate a new daycare center too.

The drive home is congested — at least what we consider congested in this area — and takes longer than I'd like. This end of Pelican Bay has seen growth in the last ten years and the streets weren't planned out to handle so much traffic. It makes even the few cars I'm sharing the road with feel like an all-out traffic jam.

Nate parked in a spot close to my building's entrance and I park beside him. Even though he already knows I lost my job, dread still fills me. Now I have to see him in person, and he'll want me to explain why I'm such a screw-up in person. I've never felt like such a loser. Why would someone as good as Nate stay with me? I'm a single mom who can't even hold down a job.

The apartment smells like an Italian grandmother stopped by and opened a restaurant. Emma wiggles to get out of my hands and I set her down, watching her trollop away in search of toys.

"You're cooking dinner?" I ask Nate, when he steps out of the kitchen holding a wooden spoon with red sauce dripping from the end.

He smiles, and his eyes travel me up and down. It wasn't that he was checking out my outfit, but since he knows the drama I've had this morning, I'm more concerned he's checking to make sure I have all my body parts. "I making my famous spaghetti. Extra cheese."

He knows I love cheese. "Why?"

I don't know why I ask because there's a million reasons he can do something nice like this. He's a good guy. He's cooked meals for me before and I've never questioned those motives. But tonight is off. This is a pity meal and I don't want Nate's pity.

I don't want anyone's pity ever again.

"Because I'm taking care of you, Josie," he says like the answer is obvious.

In the kitchen he stands by the stove, stirring a pot of red bubbling sauce.

"You don't get it, Nate. I don't need a man to take care of us. Everything was fine before you hit me."

Let's not forget I wouldn't have needed the time off work if he had paid attention in the parking lot that day rather than staring at me. It's his fault any of us are in this mess.

"Josie, I thought we were past this?"

I huff. He's right, I thought we were too, but it's been hiding in my subconscious, and today we're going to fight about it. It had to happen sooner or later.

"Why are you being this way?" he asks, giving his attention back to the pot on the stove.

Isn't it obvious? "We didn't need your help before and I don't need it now. I don't get how you cooking dinner is going to solve my problems."

Nate turns to me with an incredulous expression written on his face. "Who said spaghetti dinner had to solve all your problems? I just thought I'd feed you."

"I don't want you to feed me."

Nate rolls his eyes and goes back to stirring. "Actually, you kind of do."

"I do not. I did fine on my own before you and I will after you."

Nate's face twitches and his head tilts to the side. Annoyed. He lifts the spoon from the sauce, tapping it on the side of the pan twice before putting it in the little spoon holder in the middle of the stove. When he turns to face me, our eyes connect.

"Let me tell you something, Josie. I thought you'd gotten this by now, but we mis-communicated. Any woman I'm going to call mine will let me take care of her."

My mouth falls open in shock but he holds up a finger to silence me.

"Now, if she wants to go to work, and that's important to her, fine. I prefer she didn't, but whatever. My woman has a bad day and I want to make her dinner to help her feel better? I don't expect her to get on my case about trying to be a nice guy. She says thanks."

A second of silence spills between us and I don't comment, so Nate keeps talking.

"I mean you could pay me back later... In the bedroom. And that would be okay, but sometimes people do nice things for one another because they want to."

"I'm not your woman," I spit out.

Nate's eyes widen. "Yes, you are."

"No, I'm not and I never will be. I won't be anyone's woman ever again. I'm taking care of myself." The only person who won't let me down in life is me. There's no one else I can depend on and I won't let my heart get hurt by another guy ever again.

Nate and I stand off as our eyes glare at one another, neither of us willing to give in.

He cracks first. "Fine, that's the way you want it? To be alone?

I nod. Being alone has become my mantra. It's not an easy one to give up. Why accept help now when I've done such a wonderful job of screwing everything up on my own? There's no point in bringing Nate on my spiral downward. He still has a chance of a normal life and he should get to go out there and live it without all the added weight of my problems.

13

He dusts his hands off on the top of his pants and turns the oven burner to low. "Give the sauce another five minutes, top off the noodles, and stick it in the oven for twenty-five. I like to top it with cheese."

"Where are you going?" I ask as he stomps past the kitchen table.

"I'm letting you take care of yourself. Good luck, Josie," he says, looking back once before opening the apartment door and walking out.

The door bangs hard against the frame and Emma cries out in shock. I turn to where she sits in the living room, watching the whole scene as tears form in her eyes.

Great. I'm off to a wonderful start being my own woman.

"GIVE ME JUST A MINUTE, EMMA." Not listening, she continues yelling in the middle of the room because the television show I turned on to entertain her switched to something new. I don't know what that child has against Pirates, but she does not like them.

The toaster pops and I reach behind me to grab two slices. They're hot and burn the tips of my fingers. "Ouch," I fumble with them, dropping one piece on the floor. "You asshole."

The toast doesn't seem offended at my choice of vocabulary as I drop it in the trash. I guess it's off the menu.

The eggs in the pan on top of the stove crackle, and when I use the spatula to flip them over, most of them stick to the bottom of pan becoming a burnt brown crisp that will need to soak for days.

Why was this so easy yesterday morning and so hard today?

It's a question I don't want to answer. Today is different because it's missing one of the key components. He was also missing from my bed last night. It's a hard adjustment when you go from sleeping alone, to sleeping with someone wonderful, to sleeping alone. Not having Nate here doesn't feel right or natural.

"It's cereal for breakfast, Emma. Come on," I try to coax her to the table while dropping the scorched pan in the sink. She doesn't care at all.

I pour a bit of the sugary cereal I vowed I'd never feed my children if I had any into a bowl and top it off with milk, setting it in front of her highchair.

"Emma, come here. We need to eat."

It's not that I've anywhere special I need to be today,

but I've got things to do. I have jobs to apply for and even though I've already paid for the daycare today since they wouldn't let me out of my contract with them, I'm keeping Emma home. Not having a job wasn't a good enough excuse. I considered putting her in for the last four days, but then they called and said they'd given our opening to another client so they didn't have room. How can a daycare kick us out but still charge us? Something seems wrong with that racket.

Emma still hasn't moved from her spot on the floor, so I walk over and pick her up. She hits my back with her tiny hands, complaining about missing the princesses.

I fight with her to get her in the highchair as her feet kick out. She pulls on my hair and I struggle. Her foot kicks and connects with the bowl of cereal, flipping it and sending the milk and sugared coated marshmallows over the both of us.

"Emma!" I scold, putting her back on the floor and doing my best to stop up the milk before it gets to the carpet. They don't make spoiled milk candles for a reason. It will stink up the place if it's allowed to stay in the carpet. No one wants to wake up to that in the morning.

A second stream of milk puddles as it falls from the top of the table, and I rush off to the bathroom to get towels to soak it up.

With one hand holding the towels, trying to get as much milk as possible without crunching the cereal into the fabric, I take ten deep breaths while watching Emma stare at the television in search of her princesses.

Even with my ankle healed and no place to be this morning, I still suck at this adult thing.

My heart hurts and not just because I worry I can't make it on my own. It's also pounding because yesterday I sent away one of the best people I've ever met in my life. What's so wrong with the fact someone wanted to take care of me? Am I so jaded I can't ask for a little help from someone?

"Emma!" I yell, as she knocks off the two television remotes from the coffee table.

"Princess!" she yells back. Well, it sounds like "pin trees," but she gets the point across.

I stalk to her and grab her up from the floor, carrying her into her bedroom to change her clothes. "You don't get any princesses today." Who wants to watch some beautiful skinny chick with great hair fall for a super-rich prince who lives in a castle with servants to do all their laundry? It sets an unrealistic precedent.

Emma looks at me and her face falls as her eyes narrow and her lips pucker. She's unhappy about my decision.

I feel bad. It's not her fault my life is a mess. Every choice that got us to where we are right now is one I made. This problem is one of my making. I pat her on the back, taking off her milk-soaked shirt. "It's okay, baby. You can watch all the princesses you want in a minute."

"Princesses?" she asks.

Screw it. "We'll spend all day with the princesses."

I'm sure my mother brought her the Disney princess collection DVDs before she was out of the womb. If Emma wants a day watching the ladies in pretty dresses fall for their princes, I'm okay with that.

I'm just tired of always needing someone else. First, I had my parents, and then I moved in with my husband,

and for a few months Emma and I were here. We were doing okay on our own and then out of the blue Nate barreled into my life causing mass destruction and chaos. He's a wonderful man and a great guy. I was stupid to let him go, but I can't continue to run to somebody else every time I find myself in a little of trouble.

At some point I have to stand up, accept my life, and prove — not only to myself but to the world — that Josie Summerton can make it on her own.

I'm going to do this. I'm going to get my shit together and provide a stable home for Emma and me. And when that time comes, only then will I consider looking for someone new to share my life with. By then I'm sure Nate will have found a better woman than me to make lots of babies with. The thought threatens to tear open my heart, but I refuse to give it time to fester. I can only hope that by then I'll be able to find someone like Nate. Not as good as Nate because he is a class of his own, but maybe half as good. Even half of Nate would be better than most of the men in the entire world.

MY PHONE PINGS with a notification from the kitchen table where I left it, and my first response is to jump up from the floor where I'm organizing Emma's toys and grab it. But I don't. Yes, I hope it's Nate, but even if it is, I won't rush over there and beg him to take me back. I have standards.

It's been two days since he walked out. You don't leave a woman waiting and then text her out of the blue. So if Nate is my text message, he can stay there.

Emma and I are doing fine.

Perfectly fine.

Okay, to be 100 percent honest, we've been better. I may have survived the last two days, but they sucked. Even if Nate no longer wants to see me — which I'm fine with — we've been cooped up indoors. I, however, have applied to fifteen jobs. It may not seem like a lot, but there are not many jobs in this area. It wasn't something I thought about when I moved to Pelican Bay since I wasn't planning to get fired.

I drop the last of Emma's dolls at the bottom of the row so her purple dress was in the group with all the other purple dress dolls. It's a rather unbalanced rainbow I've created with each doll stacked in order of their color-coordinated outfit. She has no blue dolls and only one little girl not wearing a dress. It's time as a mother I work a little more variety into her playthings.

I also need to find a hobby. Take up knitting or something. The only thing I'm excelling at now is training for an Oreo eating competition. That and tracking Nate's phone location from his fancy app. He's been all over town – not missing me at all.

My phone beeps again, alerting me I hadn't read the text the first time — like I didn't already know. It takes all my strength to pull myself off the floor, but I get up and go to look.

I'm not crossing my fingers and saying a little prayer it's Nate when I swipe the screen to read the message.

Lies.

And I'm not deflated when I realize it's not.

More lies.

TABITHA: Stop by the bakery tomorrow.

Even if my short relationship with Nate didn't work out the way I wanted, at least he introduced me to Tabitha, Winnie, and Anessa. Katy too.

ME: Will Nate be there?

I've been locked away the last two days and I'm not sure what they know of Nate and my break-up situation.

TABITHA: No, and Ridge says they have handled the situation with the storage.

ME: Em and I will stop in the bakery tomorrow.

It will be nice to get out and see other people again. I forgot how boring it is being locked away indoors all day.

A knock infiltrates the quiet of my apartment and I rush to open the door so the loud banging doesn't wake Emma. There isn't much time for my heart to wish it's Nate pounding on my door, but in the split second it takes me to get there, I do.

I don't waste a second checking the peephole because if another knock wakes Emma I'll be furious. And if it is Nate, I don't want to wait. There's no reason to give him time to reconsider and run away.

The door swings open and I have a huge smile on my face that drops the second I see who's on the other side.

It's not Nate.

14

"Josie, can we talk?" she questions, acting as if I hate her enough to send her away.

I should. Any woman should have the right to say no and slam the door in the face of the person who broke up her marriage. I consider doing it, but then she sniffles and runs a Kleenex underneath her eyes, smearing her mascara. It's obvious she's been crying hard even before she made it to my door.

I step back giving her room to come in. "Sure, Lindsey. What's wrong?"

I don't even feel guilty that for a split-second I hope she is here to tell me that Barry was in a horrible car accident and was decapitated in a gruesome fashion.

Okay fine, I feel a little guilty about it. He's an asshole, but he is Emma's dad.

The skinny tall beautiful blonde who only makes me want to rip out her hair on occasion sits down at my dining room table like my house is a casual place and we're two best friends having a drink. She lays her hands down on her arms sniffling a few times.

"I think Barry is cheating on me."

I widen my eyes to look shocked and resist the urge of replying, "That wouldn't surprise me." The truth is, it wouldn't. Barry cheated on me with her. Why would she expect anything less from him now?

But even though I've spent countless nights lying in bed hoping for Karma to get them both, I've been in her shoes right now and it sucks. You love someone and trust them with your heart only for them to throw it on the ground and do a little tap dance over it. No one deserves that treatment from another human.

"What makes you think so?"

She sniffles letting her head hang. "He's worked late every night for the last two weeks. He keeps telling me he's hanging out at the bar with his friends or watching the game, but it's not true because..."

My head tilts the side. "Those are the same excuses he gave me?"

She nods. "I'm sorry. You shouldn't even listen to me, but I had nowhere else to go."

My head wobbles like my neck can't keep it up. Her apology doesn't make up for all the pain she caused me in the past, but it's more than I ever thought I'd get.

"Josie, I don't know what to do."

To be nice, I sit down in the chair across the table from her. I don't get why she wants to do anything except break up with him, but it's not my relationship. "Have you confronted him?"

Once I confronted Barry by standing at the end of our bed screaming, he spent a few minutes denying them, but he crumbled quite easily. He should never go anywhere near a witness stand.

"You know Barry. I'm scared of what he'll say. I told him now that your divorce is final, he has to marry me and he said no."

Turning my head, I chuckle and do my best to get quiet so I don't offend her. It doesn't surprise me that he won't get remarried. Our divorce wasn't what you'd call pleasant. I've never considered myself a vengeful person — at least not until he cheated — but I made my husband pay... at the bank. I don't feel guilty about it in the slightest.

He's probably learned his lesson about shared assets.

"I can't tell you what to do, Lindsey. I'm sorry. Make your own choice in how you handle it, but if you're worried, I would ask him to be honest with you. It's always better to know the truth than to wonder."

It's true. I believe every word I said. Learning my husband was a cheater sucked. It was one of the worst days of my life, but I'd rather know and get to make my own choices than go through life wondering.

"Do you think he'll ever marry me?" she asks, her tears picking up as she wipes them away with the tissue.

I shake my head. "Maybe. He has a crazy ex-wife who took him for a lot of money in his last divorce. He might be ring shy. Give him some time."

Lindsey smiles up at me, even though it fades as she nods her head. Right then, as I'm looking into her sad but beautiful blue eyes, I realize I'm not angry anymore. Sure, I'm still hurt — and probably always will be — but I'd rather live the life I'm living right now than still be with my ex. And I'm sorry he's continuing his shitty behavior with new women. If he is in fact cheating. Who knows with Barry?

I reach across the table and pat the top of her hands. "If he is cheating on you, Lindsey, he is stupid."

"I know, right?" she says, followed by a laugh when she realizes what she said. "He keeps getting awesome women and then treating us like crap and we keep going back."

Not all of us go back, I want to say, but I refrain. It's not the time. She has to get there on her own.

"You're right. I'm going to go home and ask him what's going on. I deserve better than this."

I stand when she does and walk her to the door. "Just make sure and ask three times so you get the truth. He's like that character from the *Austin Powers* movies."

Lindsey looks at me and blinks, not understanding a word I've said. Oh youth. They missed out on so many wonderful movies.

"Right, you're way too young for *Austin Powers*. Push him a little. He might deny it first, but he'll cave in the end."

She nods her head, sturdy and strong with a new resolution. I watch Lindsey walk out the door and down my hallway with her back held straight. She's a girl on a mission.

I spend another second locking up behind her then fifteen of them tapping my fingernails on the kitchen table before I realized that, like Lindsey, I'm stupid. Rather than admit my problems and what worried me the other day, I lashed out at Nate. It wasn't his fault I lost my job.

He'd done nothing wrong but want to support me, which is what you should want in a relationship. But because I've never been in a good one, I freaked out. I used Barry's shortcomings against Nate and that's not fair. Nate is three times the man my ex has ever been and would ever be.

And I was stupid and let him walk out my door. When you find something great, you don't throw it away. You cultivate it with love and kindness. Grow it to be even better.

I let the best man in Pelican Bay go and now all I can hope is he hasn't found someone to replace me in the two days he's been a fish back out in the sea. Pelican Bay is crawling with women looking to hook themselves an ex-military type.

I'll never forgive myself if I lose Nate because of my stupid behavior. Screw standards. It's time to win him back.

My cell phone is inches away from where I dropped it after texting with Tabitha, and I grab it pulling up Nate's number. I consider the pretty women I've seen in Pelican Bay and a frantic side of me takes over, wanting to get my call through as fast as possible before some other woman puts her hooks in him. She could be reeling him in as I pace with the phone to my ear.

"Josie?" he asks, when he answers the phone.

I'm out of breath, worried about what to say and also trying to think as quickly as possible. "Nate! Are you at home?"

I cross my fingers he's not at the bar.

"Yes," he answers hesitantly.

A worst fear comes to mind. "Is there anyone else

there?" I ask, my heart threatening to break open my chest.

"No, is everything okay? You're being weird."

"We need to talk."

"Okay, I'll come right over."

"Right now?" This conversation can't wait until tomorrow. It has to happen tonight. If we wait, I might lose my gumption.

Nate breathes into the phone. "I'll be right there. Sit tight."

I hang up the phone and glimpse what I'm wearing — a pair of grey sweatpants and an oversized University of Maine sweatshirt. This won't work.

With newfound energy I never possess after dinner, I make it to my bedroom and swap out the outfit for ripped jeans and a tight, but not too tight pink blouse I like to wear for job interviews.

I stop in front of the mirror and check out my outfit. Shit. This won't work. He'll question why I'm dressed up again going to a job interview at nine o'clock at night. I have to be smooth, calm, unassuming. Pretend like I haven't been affected by him being gone the last two days.

In the end, there is no time for an outfit change because Nate doesn't stop and knock at the door. He walks right in like he's always done.

How did I forget he has a key?

"Josie?" He yells, in a quiet whisper into the apartment.

I dart out of my bedroom cursing the outfit choice. "Coming."

Nate meets me in the hallway. "Is everything okay? You sounded upset on the phone."

With a deep breath, I go for it. I hug him, clutching to his chest like I'm scared if I let go he'll fade away, but eventually I have to drop my hands and take a step back so I can face Nate.

"Nate, I was upset. I'm stupid and I'm so sorry for what I said on Monday. It was only because I was upset over losing my job and they kicked Emma out of daycare."

His eyebrows pinch together. "They kicked *my* Emma out of daycare?" I refuse to believe his use of "my Emma" means he still has feelings for us. I can't get my hopes up.

"Yes, but it's a long story." I don't want to get into it right now. "I'm sorry and I miss you. I would like us to get back to where we were before." Before I went stupid and ruined everything. I leave that part out.

Nate stares at me... and blinks... and then he stares at me more. What he doesn't do is start talking.

Oh screw it. The hopes are up that he'll accept my apology and we'll live happily ever after.

After what feels like a decade, he shakes his head no. "I'm sorry, Josie."

My heart crumbles. All the wishes and dreams and hopes I had for us break down and fly away in the slight breeze when the central air kicks on.

My worst fears come true. I pushed away the best thing that's ever happened to me since having Emma. I tossed the best guy the world has ever seen. The best one I stood a chance with. If I can't make it work with Nate, there's no hope for me in the future.

15

"You broke my heart, Josie. All I wanted to do was be there for you and you pushed me away like I didn't mean anything."

"You mean the world to me, Nate. I was being stupid and emotional."

"And what happens the next time you have a bad day? Would you do it again?"

"Never," I promise.

He shakes his head no again. "I just don't know, Josie. You brought me into your house and I got attached to Emma and you. I don't want to go back and forth. If I'm here, I want to be here forever."

I reach for his chest but he steps back. "I want you here forever, Nate."

He takes another step back, putting even more distance between us. "I need some time to think about it. You did a number on me and I spent the last few days thinking about how not to let that happen again."

"It won't happen again."

"You told me you wanted to be an independent woman and I don't want to take that chance away from you," he says, halfway back to the door.

I don't know what to say to make him stay. Or if there even is anything I could say to stop the destruction from happening.

"I'm so sorry, Nate. Can you think about it and let us talk through this problem?"

He drops his head, staring at the carpet, and when he lifts it again, I see his answer. It's written all over his face as clear as if the words were spelled out on his forehead in permanent ink.

"No."

I nod. If I had something I could tell him, a promise I could make, I would. But just like I couldn't save Lindsey's relationship, I can't save my own.

"I'll call you in a few days," Nate says as he stands in the doorway, half in my apartment and half out. And then without another world he turns and walks out. I watch him leave, his back tall and straight as he strides his way down the hallway never once looking back to see the pain written on my face.

IN MY GRANDMOTHER'S house when I was growing up, she had an old rotary phone hanging on the wall. When I would spend weekends at her house and friends would call, I could lie on the floor with my feet kicked up on the wall dangling the cord around my fingers as we talked. I've never wished for a corded phone so much as when I'm on the phone with my mother.

It would give me something to do because if she hears me make any noise in the background of our conversation, she'll assume she's bothering me and then launch into the talk about how children these days can't just enjoy a phone conversation. We always have to be doing something else. It's less of a bother to just wander around aimlessly than try to use my time effectively.

"Did you hear me, Josie?" my mother asks, and I put down the magazine I've been mindlessly flipping through. If she's going to ask difficult questions, I better pay attention.

"Of course, Mom. No, I don't have a job yet it's only been four days."

"Well, you'd have more opportunities here."

I stand from the table and walk a circle around Emma as she plays on the floor. "Yes, I realize there are more jobs in Bangor."

"Our home is always open to you. It would be the smart place to figure out your life now, Josie."

My left eye twitches and I slam the eyelid down to stop it in its tracks. We had this conversation so many times after the divorce. "No, Mom, I'm not moving back in with you and Dad."

My brain isn't even capable of processing the horror that would be. I made it through eighteen years of life with only small mental damage. I can't do any more time in my mother's house without risking further compromise.

"You don't have to be all pissy about it. I'm just suggesting that we're here if you need us. I can't have one of my children living on the street. What would the girls say?"

I shake my head, sitting on the couch and then lying down with one foot propped up on the back portion. It's not as good as the wall at my grandmother's home where I used to sit for hours with a phone clutched to my ear talking to a classmate, but it will do. "I don't know, Mother. What *would* the girls say?" I'm a long way from living on the streets. Mostly.

"Well now you're just being unbearable."

I make a mistake of lifting my left eyelid and it twitches again.

My phone beeps, so I hold it out from my ear to catch the small green bar at the top that flashes with an incoming call.

"Oh, Mom, I've got to go. Someone is calling and you never know. It could be a job interview."

"Don't you have call waiting on your cell phone?"

"Of course, but I have no idea how to use it." I've never successfully switched between calls on my phone. Has anybody?

"Fine, take the call. But if it is the job, call me back right away and we can talk about interviewing techniques," says the woman who's never interviewed for a job in her life.

I sigh but agree, anything to get her off the phone.

The problem with my cell phone — besides the fact I barely know how to use it — is that when you switch over to a new call, you can't see who it is. I hate not knowing who is on the phone. But I wasn't lying when I said it could be a call for an interview. It can also be my ex or his girlfriend calling to give me an update on their situation, which I'd rather not hear, but I have to take the chance.

"Hello?" I ask, after hitting the green bar to accept the call.

There's silence along with a smattering of static and then, "Josie?" Nate says. "Why do you sound weird?"

I sit up ramrod straight on the couch. This was not the phone call I expected. "Hey, I was talking to my mother on her line. I didn't expect you to call."

"Well, I said I'd call," he replies, possibly a tinge of regret in his voice.

"Yes, but I didn't imagine it right now." I leave out the part where I add in "or ever." A lot of guys say they'll call but not many do.

"If Winnie comes over to sit with Emma for a few minutes, could you meet me in Pelican Bay?"

I pucker my lips while I stare at Emma playing on the ground and messing up her rainbow-colored blocks. "I guess. Is it important?"

I don't want to go to Pelican Bay to spend time with another man who didn't find me good enough. It's one thing to make mistakes but another thing to have them lobbed at you all day long.

"Very important. I'll meet you in the elementary school parking lot in twenty-five minutes. Okay?"

"Okay, but I need more time." It's a twenty-minute drive to Pelican Bay and I don't even know if Winnie is at home, much less if she can watch Emma. I can't just drop my child off on someone else in the blink of an eye.

Nate's voice crackles. "It's taken care of. I'll see you then," he finishes and then the line goes dead.

With the call disconnected, I release a huge breath of air, letting it run between my lips noisily. "I guess here goes nothing, Emma." She doesn't even look up to acknowledge the craziness of our current situation.

I haven't even gotten off the couch when there's a knock at the door and it slips open. "Josie, it's me."

Winnie takes a step into my apartment waving her hands. I don't know when we moved from a friendly knock to a best friend door open, but surprisingly that's the least of my worries today.

"Did Nate call you?" I ask suspiciously.

Winnie smiles, her lips pressed together, but I can tell she has a secret. "He may have suggested you would need some help with Emma, and you know how much I love Emma."

"I don't want to bother you." She's playing so well I could take her with me to Pelican Bay.

Winnie doesn't listen and walks right past me to sit on the floor with Emma. "I love her. And besides, Huxley may come over later and I want him to have as much baby time as possible."

My eyes narrow. "Does he need a lot of baby time?" Is Winnie expecting something she hasn't told the rest of us?

Her face blushes. "No, but I'm trying to work him into the idea."

"Uh-huh," I say and nod.

Winnie checks her watch as if she's wearing one, but she's only staring at her naked wrist. "You better get going. You only have about twenty minutes and you need to be in Pelican Bay."

"I can't go like this," I say, looking down at my pair of ripped jeans and a tight NIN concert T-shirt. When Nate sees me for the first time, I need to look glamorous as a real reminder of what he's missing out on now that he's not in our lives anymore. The problem is I don't own any ball gowns, but I could look better in a pair of slacks and a nice black blouse. Maybe show a little cleavage.

Winnie shakes her head. "There's no time. You look great. Just go for it."

"Do you know what this is about?" I ask because it's obvious she does.

Winnie smiles and then tries very hard not to smile by pressing her lips together. She says no, but I don't believe it for a second. "I have no idea. He only called and asked if I would be willing to babysit for a few hours."

"A few hours?" What could we possibly do in the parking lot of an elementary school for that long?

I don't bother asking again because I don't think she'll answer.

"Fine..." I say, drawing it out like a teenager being asked to do the dishes.

The drive to Pelican Bay has never felt so long... and so short. I try not to obsess over why Nate could be making me meet him at an elementary school, but I can't come up with anything. Maybe he plans to walk into the school gymnasium and dump a bucket of pig's blood on me. At this point in my life anything is possible. At least *Carrie* had cool psychic powers.

My emotions while driving go from half expecting the worst and brief moments of joy to hoping he'll pull an eighties movie reconciliation and show up with a boom-box. But of the two of us, I should make the grand gestures. Even though they wouldn't be enough to make up for what I've done.

Seeing Nate now will break my heart again. It hasn't

had a chance to heal from the last time. He's already rejected me earlier this week. Why does he feel the need to crush me once more? Regardless of how I expect this meeting to go, I can't trample the piece of my heart wishing this will be our chance to make up. A tiny piece of hope holds on that this time he'll listen to my apology.

The parking lot is empty except for a single white four-door car at the far end. Everyone is gone over summer break, so it's easy to spot Nate behind the wheel. I park my car next to his and turn it off, getting out when he leaves his car.

"Where's the truck?" I ask after deciding it's a harmless question, which won't cause my heart to leap out of my chest in despair. Probably.

He doesn't look right not driving his big oversized tires. Ones I swear are half the size my body.

He smiles. "Traded it in for this model." He taps the white car on the trunk. "It's going to take a bit to get used to."

I nod but I'm never going get used to seeing Nate riding in the baby car. It's just not right. He's not a car person.

"Did you need help with something?" I ask, trying to get this meeting over with quicker than the few hours he told Winnie I'd need a babysitter. "I don't want to keep Winnie babysitting too long." Plus seeing him and being close is painful. He's everything I could have had standing right in front of me, but yet he's not mine and I can't touch him. And it's all my fault.

My self-loathing side kicks in and I want to ask him a million questions. Has he found someone new already?

Does he miss me like I miss the hell out of him? Does he realize I'm sorry? Does he not care?

Nate shakes his head. "You know Winnie will watch Emma all day."

"Yes," I say putting a hand on my hip and trying to ward off his smile. "But I don't want to make her."

"Let's take a walk," he says, turning to the area behind him and walking onto the sidewalk.

I follow. "A walk? You want to walk?" Now?

"That's what I said." His steps are big but not because he walks quickly. Rather his long legs eat up space faster than my short ones do.

We hit the end of the sidewalk and Nate turns. "How are things going with Emma?"

"Fine…" I say, drawing the word out, but this time in a completely different way. I have no idea what we're doing and I don't like not knowing things.

Nate talks about how Spencer brought his dog into the office yesterday and she chewed up one of the office chairs. I wasn't that impressed, considering I've heard stories of other things Spencer's dog, Frankie, has eaten. But then he mentioned the chair was metal and I gained a newfound respect.

"Here we are," Nate says, stopping in front of the house.

It's a house I remember well, but I hadn't realized we were headed in that direction.

"You brought me here?" So, it's going to be a painful meeting then because standing right in before us is the beacon of everything I want in my life. Everything I want but can't have. Nate has led me right to the adorable little yellow house I tried to buy — the one I wanted, but someone else purchased right out from under me.

It's like I'm being featured on one of those "this is your life" shows, but it's full of all the wonderful things I've lost out on.

I want to be angry, yell even, but I don't have it in me. I'm too tired. Life has kicked me one too many times. Nate stands to the side, smiling at the house like an evil villain who gets pleasure out of seeing the despair of his enemy.

"You get this is the house I tried to buy. Right?" I ask without any humor. Is he so clueless?

He nods. "We should go see if there's anyone inside," he says, and the next thing I notice he's standing on top of the porch with his hands on the door opening it.

"Nate!" I yell, walking after him. "Someone else bought this house." I can't believe he's walking in without knocking. We'll get arrested on trespassing charges. Damn, I really know how to pick the men I fall in love with. That's for sure.

He spins, rounding on me after he passes through the front door. "Yeah, me."

16

I shake my head, confused. "You what?"

"I bought this house. For me... Well, for you," he says, watching my facial expressions when he drops the news.

I'm slow to pick it up. "You bought a house?"

"For you."

"A house?" This house?

"Well for us, but then you dumped me so..."

"Wait, you bought *this* house?"

Nate nods, but slowly, his enthusiasm lost.

"I knew from the minute I saw you I wanted you in my life, Josie. And then the accident happened," I don't miss how he glosses over hitting me with his truck, but I let him. "And I got to meet Emma and be a part of your life and it made me realize that's what I want. I want a family. My own family. But you wanted this house, and I heard you were having problems getting the loan. I couldn't let you lose this place after everything else. I bought it that day."

"That day?" How did he get a mortgage so fast?

He grins, ignoring my question about when and launches into other aspects. "It's a great house. Close enough to the schools that the kids can walk every day. The backyard is big enough for them to play in and host barbecues."

I nod because I know all these things. They were the reasons I loved the house, too.

He spins and my eyes follow his along the dark-grained hardwood floors and the white cut-out fireplace I was sure with a little elbow grease I could get back to the original brick color. You can't see it from where we stand, but beyond our spot there's a small dining room and then a kitchen with doors that lead out to the backyard. It's easy to imagine the whole place fixed up and I spend a second picturing a family growing here. Someone else's family.

"I want all of that, Josie. The kids, the barbecues, this house."

"But not with me," I say even though it hurts. "I tried to get you back, but you don't want me anymore because I'm a dumbass."

Nate smiles. "No, I just wanted to wait and surprise you with this house. You needed proof you weren't just an easy relationship for me. There is no end for us, Josie. I want the whole thing with you and Emma. This house is to show my commitment. If you'll have me."

Now he's gone mad, but his words become puzzle pieces and fall into place.

"You bought a house for me?" I ask, smiling and turning back in his direction. Is it enough to think maybe, possibly, he could love me?

My eyes widen as Nate nods. "I loved you from minute one, Josie."

I laugh. The tension I've carried around with me for days flows away just being in Nate's presence and knowing we're going to be okay. "You could have just told me. You didn't have to go and hit me with your truck."

"Now she tells me," he says, rolling his eyes.

Even though he said the words, he hasn't come closer, so I close the distance between us and wrap my arms around his middle. "I'm so sorry, Nate. It's just I was scared, and I didn't know what to do. After everything that's happened, I hate feeling like I don't have control of my life."

He squeezes me tightly. "You never have to feel that way ever again."

"I've been strong for so long on my own. I don't know how to accept help."

Nate leans down, kissing me on the head and trailing a finger across my jaw. "Well, I find it's easiest if you just do everything I say and don't question my decisions."

I laugh as his lips lower and we connect for the last first time.

"Do you like it?" Nate asks, a hint of nervousness in his voice.

"Yes, I love it. I was going to buy it." The house isn't huge — most of the homes aren't in Pelican Bay — but the light shines in from the large window of the living room all the way to the kitchen. The staircase leading to the second level is old and weathered, but in a way, it gives a nice patina and there's the traditional banister I wanted.

Nate places a kiss to the left of my eye where I hadn't realized it had grown wet.

"I've never had anyone buy me a house before. Are you sure?"

"I'm sure and I'll buy you a lot more than a house."

I tilt my head to look him in the eyes. They're beautiful, I'll never get enough staring at them. "Of course you're sure, but I don't want you to think I'm doing this because of the house." I wanted Nate back before he bought me a house in Pelican Bay. I don't want him to consider me some kind of gold digger.

He laughs. "I figured I'd probably upset you, but I wanted to wait until I had everything finalized. I want us to start a life together right now."

"Right... right now?" I ask, with a gleam in my eye.

Nate's gaze spans the empty room. "We should break in every room, and it would be easiest to do the living room right now."

My eyes widen, looking at the nice glossy hardwood floors beneath us. "Right now."

"Unless you have other ideas."

"No, right now is good."

Nate slips his fingers under the waistband of my pants.

"Right here?" I ask, looking out the front window that's not covered by blinds or curtains.

"Baby, I would do you anywhere."

I laugh in nervousness until it dies off as Nate pinches my nipple between two of his fingers.

I moan and he smiles. "Take off your pants."

My eyes dart to the large front window again and I

grab him by the hand, pulling him into a small corner that's more hidden next to the fireplace.

Nate shakes his head.

"What? Haven't you heard about Pearl? We don't want the whole town to know." They have cameras.

In the little alcove, Nate pushes me against the wall and pops the button on my pants. They fall to the floor and his hand snakes down into my underwear.

I guess we're doing this quick.

Not that I'm complaining.

I moan and rub myself against his hand harder. He pushes his head under my shirt getting high enough next to my chest he can lick the top of my breasts.

My head bumps against the wall as I lean back, enjoying what he does to me.

Until it all stops. My eyes pop open and I look into Nate's as he moves his head and stares back at me wordlessly.

"I don't have a condom."

My body deflates. "You didn't bring one with you?" I guess former SEALS no longer follow the "always be prepared" motto. Or maybe that's the Boy Scouts.

He looks ashamed for a second. "I've had a lot on my mind the last few days."

"I'm on the pill, so I'm okay if we... You know," I say looking at the area of his pants where his cock pushes tightly against his jeans.

He considers it. "I'm swear I'm clean but I can get a test if you want."

I smile. "No, I trust you."

He blows out a breath in glee. "Thank fuck."

His jeans come off and he tears my shirt from my

chest, the cool air of the house tightening my nipples when he exposes them by slipping off my bra.

"Missed you," he says, taking a nipple in his mouth and sucking.

"Oh my word, Nate," I say, banging my head back against the wall. My hand grabs on to the elastic of his boxers. I try to pull him closer, but his fingers slip into my opening and frazzle my wits.

Nate steps back, dislodging my hand from his pants. "I can't wait, babe. I'm sorry. I need to be in you." He slips himself free and then wraps one of my legs around his hips, stepping away to place my back against the wall. He glides easily inside and my pussy clenches around him. I've missed him too.

"Don't wait," I say when he doesn't start moving.

Nate chuckles, running his chin stubble across my neck and placing kisses on my collarbone. "I like it when you're greedy."

He doesn't waste time, setting a steady rhythm right from the beginning as he works to fill me deeper and deeper each time our bodies come together. His fingers slip between our bodies and rub circles on my clit.

I arch my back, pushing my shoulders against the wall and doing my best to get as close to him as possible. The tightness builds in my body quickly and I dig my fingers into his shoulders holding on.

"Faster," I demand.

He listens, pumping into me harder. His fingers sink into my ass cheeks as he moves my body up and down on his cock. The stretched feeling fills my entire being with all that Nate gives me.

"That's right, baby. Take it."

My body clenches and my toes curl as my legs draw him closer.

"Nate," I gasp out.

He picks up speed, hammering into me quicker. Then his fingers tug at my swollen clit, which causes me to jump and lose control, the orgasm taking over when I'm unprepared. I scream, pushing my head against the wall until it hurts as Nate slows and his cum fills me.

When he stops, he places his forehead against mine as our hearts beat as one. My legs stop twitching when he pulls himself from my body and sets me on the ground, wiping a hand between my legs and sticking two fingers his mouth. Nate smiles and I blush not believing what I'm seeing.

"We are going to have so much fun christening this house."

I laugh. Living the rest of my life with Nate sure will be interesting.

"Is there any furniture you're attached to?" Nate asks as he watches me buckle my seatbelt in his brand-new pristine car.

If he's serious about this whole being in a relationship thing — which I think he is — I can never let him drive Emma anywhere. His backseat will be full of crackers and melted M&Ms. The commercials lie. They do melt in your hand if you're under the age of five.

My attention goes from the pristine back seat, with the light tan leather upholstery, to the furniture in my apartment. I bought it used and from a thrift store, but I love it. Although, the couch has two holes in one cushion that I hide strategically with throw pillows.

"My furniture sucks. We can use yours."

Nate puts the car in drive and pulls out of the parking lot. "Mine is worse. What if we bought new?"

"All new furniture?"

He nods.

"Furniture can be expensive." Especially when I'm picking it out. I remember back to my previous life when I'd been married and had a more open budget. I once spent six thousand dollars on a living room set. I had no idea back then.

"Don't worry about it," he says.

How can I not worry about it? My entire life is built around worry. I have a child. Worrying is the one part of motherhood I might actually be successful at.

"Did you sign for the house? When are you moving in?"

Nate looks to me and I swear his eyes call me crazy. "*We're* moving in as soon as possible."

"But I have a lease, and breaking it will be expensive." I can't remember what my lease said, but it has to be a few months' rent. It's not that I'm against living with Nate, but I can't pack up and move as fast as he can. I have commitments, attachments, signed legally binding contracts.

Nate slows the car stop at a stop sign. "Are you having second thoughts?" He places his hand on my knee.

"Absolutely not," I promise because it's the truth. "This is a lot of stuff to plan. I didn't have much notice." There're loads of lists to make. Timelines. Movers. And packing. I don't have any boxes.

Nate squeezes my knee reassuringly. "Don't worry, Josie. I'll take care of everything. We'll handle it one step at a time."

"One step at a time?" That will take years.

He nods like he's not worried at all about how we'll figure it out. "I want to hire some people to come in and paint the house first, so it'll probably be a week or two before we can move in."

He's going to pay for movers and painters?

"You can't pay someone to paint, Nate. I don't have a job. I can paint."

He shakes his head. "Josie, it'll be fine."

"But it's a lot of money."

He pulls in front of a building on the opposite side of Main Street in downtown Pelican Bay. It's a block I haven't visited yet because it is not down the main strip and most people don't have a reason to go unless they're looking for the hot guy who works at the hardware. I've heard a lot about him from the ladies.

Nate shuts the car off and pats my leg. "I have a lot of money."

"You do?"

"I was a single guy in the military on high-risk missions who had no life or girlfriend for years. Without housing, food, or any expenses, I've managed to save most of my money and I also made some good investments." He smiles at the last bit and I want to ask more, but there's no time when he opens the door and steps out of the car.

"Where are we going?" I ask, following him.

Let's be honest, this man could lead me into a burning house and I'd follow along with a smile.

"I have to stop by the office right quick. Ridge said one of his outside contractors is stopping by this morning with information."

We walk up to a building. The glass front door has Pelican Bay Security etched on it but nothing else.

The inside of the building is boring — a place like you'd expect a bunch of men to work. There's lots of grey and not a single potted plant to be found.

There's a reception desk with a woman sitting behind it filing a long red fingernail. She looks up as we walk in and smiles in my direction.

"You're Nate's woman?"

Nate nods. "Be nice."

The receptionist rolls her eyes and points to the hallway behind her. "They're waiting for you."

Nate's eyes flicker between her and me, and then he grabs ahold of my hand, wrapping our fingers together as he shuffles me down the hallway with him.

It's not until we're passed it when I realized the front desk was empty. Not a phone or computer in sight. Just a lone woman with her nail file.

"Nate," Ridge says, stepping out in the hallway from the room. He closes the door behind him when he sees me. "Lukis is in here with the intel, but he brought someone with him and she's in the conference room. I'm sure she could use a friend to chat with, if you know what I mean?"

Ridge tilts his head in my direction indicating I should be said friend.

"Are you okay with that?" Nate asks.

"Sure."

Nate deposits me in a large open room full of

windows and the biggest table I have never seen in real life. It would fit twenty people although I only count sixteen chairs.

"Hey, they sent you to babysit me," the redhead at the head of the table says, typing away on her cell phone.

I look around. "Or you're supposed to babysit me. I'm not sure which. I *have* gotten in trouble lately."

She laughs. "It's not life until you have a little trouble. Right?"

"I don't know." There's been a lot of trouble since I moved to Pelican Bay.

"I saw the guy who dropped you off, and it's best to keep these men on their toes. Trust me. I have one of my own."

"Where are you from?" I don't know everyone in Pelican Bay, but I feel like her fiery red hair would set her apart from others.

She stares in the corner of the ceiling as if my question is hard. "Most recently, riding around with Lukis. Causing mischief and getting on his nerves. I'm Hannah."

I take her hand when she reaches across the table to shake mine. "Josie."

"So, this office building is hot guy central and they all walk around with permanent scowls on their faces kind of like my Lukis. Are all the men who work for Ridge like this?"

I picture Nate's beautiful smile and the fact he rarely ever scowls. "I think it's only some of them."

"Lukis is bossy and acts like he knows what's best for me, but I think I may be falling for him."

"You guys been together a long time?"

Hannah giggles. "Like a week. The length of time it takes to drive here from Las Vegas."

"Oh." That is fast. "Sometimes you just know." It didn't take me long with Nate.

Hannah sighs, her eyes dreamy. "Yup, sometimes it's obvious. After this we're headed up to Wisconsin to see one of his buddies and then who knows from there."

"You just travel around together?"

"For now. I used to have a job, but Lukis works freelance and goes were he's needed. I don't plan to let him out of my sight, so I guess that's means I'm along for the ride."

"What does he do for Ridge?"

She shrugs. "I don't know. But it involves guns, the mob, and papers with a lot of dates on them. Once we had those, we hightailed it here, and he wasn't great about answering questions."

I take a minute to visualize what her life must be like. And fail.

I can't imagine what it would be like to live out of a truck and drive around the United States. Sounds dreadful, but from the way Hannah talks and how her facial expressions change when Lukis is brought up, I have a feeling she loves every minute of their time together.

It seems I'm not the only one in Pelican Bay who is falling hard and fast for a former SEAL. Maybe everyone is right, and it really does happen this quickly. When you know, you know.

And right now sitting in an oversized conference room with someone I've never met before but who seems as in love with her man as I am with mine, I realize it's true. I absolutely do love Nate. The emotions hit me like a brick and I smile. The fear and worry about having the two of us move in together fades away because all that matters is we're together. It doesn't matter how long it takes to get there or how hard the journey is. We'll be together and that's the important part of our equation.

"HAS IT BEEN A MONTH ALREADY?" Nate asks as I stack a multitude of clothes in the overnight bag for Emma.

I stop while folding a light sweater. It's the middle of the summer, but she might get cold. I finish folding the little sleeves in and tuck it in the bag. "Don't remind me. The time between Emma's father's visits seems to get shorter every month."

The only difference this month is while I'm nervous, I'm not as worried as I normally am. It's more of a distinction. Nate and my relationship is going well since my big screwup. I have spent most of my free time painting the new house. I refused to let him hire painters when I'm jobless and have working arms. Nate makes Emma and me breakfast and then goes off to a day at work. It would be rather normal if I wasn't aware of the fact that working for Nate is spying on the town's motorcycle club or watching a bazillion cameras keeping track of Pelican Bay's citizens as they buy cupcakes.

Talk about big brother. Pelican Bay has about thirty of them when you consider Ridge's forces. With Emma gone this weekend, it seemed the perfect time to do the big push to get all of our belongings to the new house. In a little under twenty-four hours I will leave this tiny apartment behind and take up residence in a new life with

Nate and the cute little house a block away from Emma's future school.

Sending Emma off today — while scary — isn't as bad as it could be because when I get my baby back, our future will be bright and we'll be off to a new adventure.

There's a knock at the door — presumably my ex — and Nate tenses before he turns, acting like plans to walk to the living room and answer it.

I pull him back. "Nate, let me handle this."

17

Barry didn't seem keen about having to pick Emma up and drop her off again this month. He was even less excited about it when I explained we needed the extra help because we were moving. I don't need him and Nate to get into an argument in front of Emma. Hopefully he got his yelling done over the phone.

Nate scowls but takes a deep breath and hands Emma to my waiting arms after I loop her bag over my shoulder.

"I'll be right back," I say and kiss him on his cheek.

Emma giggles and babbles on about her dad as we walk to the front door together, her bouncing on my hip. "You're going to be good for your daddy. Right?" I ask and she smiles. "But not too good."

I whisper the last encouragement so her father doesn't hear.

She's all smiles as I open the door and even yells out "Daddy" when she sees him. But both of our faces fall when we get an eyeful of Barry's expression. His eyes are already narrowed and his lips pursed together in annoyance. I guess he assumes I took too long. He always had a corn cob up his butt at the slightest inconvenience.

His eyes search the visible space in my apartment, stopping just a second on each box. "So it's true, then?"

It doesn't take a genius to figure out what his anger pertains to. "Yes," I say doing my best not to roll my eyes. "I don't know why you would think I'd lie about moving."

"Half the things you do I think you only do to annoy me, Josie. Who knows what the truth is?"

He's in a pleasant mood. Not.

"Just please remember when you drop her off we'll be at the new house. I texted you the address."

"Fucking A, Josie, I just can't believe you would be so irresponsible to move in with someone this quickly. I expected better from you," he says, his pissed off facial expression miraculously never changing.

For a second I consider asking if he's had Botox, but it's not a good time. Although I've heard if you make a face while getting Botox is sticks like that for hours, so it could explain his current situation.

"If I recall, you moved in with Lindsey quickly." I would call her *The Whore* but after our session a few weeks ago, I feel she deserves a name. "How is she doing?" she never called to give me an update, and I never searched one out.

Barry rolls his eyes. "That situation is different. Emma already had a relationship with Lindsey."

My eyes widen and I have to swallow back anger so I don't lose my cool in front of Emma. I do a little bit anyway. "Yeah, because she was the babysitter!" Why has he never understood his own bullshit?

He doesn't respond and I'm left standing in my doorway shaking my head and questioning why I ever cried a single tear over him. I hand Emma to her Nimrod of a father along with her overnight bag and practice deep breathing so I don't argue with him more. It's never worth it. Barry has never seen his part in our divorce and he never will. It's about time I give up the fight.

Barry struggles to hold Emma and her bag — he doesn't have as much practice — and without even a goodbye from him he barely gives me time to kiss Emma twice and wave to her as he walks down the hallway. A hand settles on my shoulder and I turn, greeted with Nate's chest. I lean my head against his pecs and watch as the two of them walk away.

"Co-parenting with him will be so much fun."

Nate's body shakes for a moment and then he places a soft kiss on top of my head. "We'll make it work."

I smile as Emma's form disappears when they turn the corner, not because my baby is leaving for the weekend, but because I believe Nate. Even if Barry continues his asshole behavior for the rest of his life, somehow Nate and I will work through it together. For Emma's sake.

"WHY IS THERE an entire box labeled 'Emma shoes'?" One of the guys who Nate invited over asks as he stops in front of Tabitha and me at the kitchen table.

I stumble over my words, not sure how to explain that every time I see a cute pair of shoes, I buy them. My child will have enough footwear to get her through high school.

"You don't ask a woman about her delicates," Tabitha says, jumping in to save the day.

The man — I'm pretty sure he was introduced as Elliot — looks down at the box and then up at Tabitha and then down to the box again. "Never mind. I don't want to know."

Tabitha shakes her head like it's a job well done as he turns and carries the box out of my apartment.

Katy smacks her gum, not taking her eyes off the retreating man's butt. "If I had known they were all like this, I would've started showing up to these things a lot more. That's a heavy box. Look at those muscles."

Tabitha covers her friend's eyes. "Don't look at that one. He's taken by me," she says laughing as Katy pushes her hand down while Ridge walks by carrying a box. He winks in Tabitha's direction and she sighs, her eyes falling to her large engagement ring as he walks out the door.

Katy looks to me. "If I'm ever that ridiculous over a man, please take me out back and shoot me."

"Okay," I agree laughing, hoping I never have to do anything of the sort.

"You can look at that one," Tabitha says as Crispin walks by. "He's single."

"Have you and Ridge decided when you'll tie the knot?" Katy asks, her eyes following Crispin as her tongue rubs across her top lip. "I've seen that one. He's pleasant but not... preppy enough. Too much stubble."

Tabitha's eyes fall to the ring again. "I think the spring. If we start planning now, we can have a wedding together by then."

"I hope you're prepared to invite the whole town to

the reception." Katy leans to the side so she doesn't lose her view of Crispin walking away. She doesn't appear too upset over his stubble from this angle.

"Absolutely not. I want a small intimate affair, maybe thirty people."

"A small wedding would be beautiful in the spring," I say, thinking of the little white chapel in town.

Katy shakes her head. "You are marrying Ridge Jefferson. *The Ridge Jefferson*. Everyone expects an invitation. The whole town wants to witness the event."

"You think so?" Tabitha asks hesitantly.

Katy nods. "Do you know he once dated and dumped a girl because he said she was obsessed with her nails?"

"What does that mean?" I ask.

Katy and Tabitha both shake their heads. They have no idea. "Believe me when I say it's not even the most ridiculous reason Ridge broke up with someone in the past. Our friend Tabitha here is the only one who's ever been able to keep him. And now she's marrying him. The whole town wants pictures."

"We'll put an announcement in the paper."

Katy smiles a little wickedly. "Girl, this shit will make the front page of the paper."

Tabitha's face falls into a mixture of shock and horror. "Can they do that?"

"If you live in Pelican Bay, they can."

The living room having been placed into boxes, Nate walks out from the hallway and stops where we've gathered.

"This is the last one from the bedrooms. I think we're ready to go."

Behind him, five guys stand, each of them wearing matching black polo shirts.

"Thank you so much." The thought of hiring movers and paying for them was almost scarier than thinking of having to move all these boxes ourselves. But Nate said when you're in Ridge's family you have lots of help. They don't even bring over the whole crew, just Nate, Crispin, and a few stragglers.

There wasn't much furniture in the apartment anyway, and most of what I had we donated to neighbors. So they didn't even need all five of the big black trucks they dedicated to the cause. I kept Emma's crib and my favorite bedside table, but everything else furniture-wise in the new house is new. It makes the moving easier.

"Don't worry about it. Anything for Nate's woman," Crispin says, slapping Nate on the back of his shoulder.

I blush. In the past being called someone's woman would be completely un-feminist, but something about being *Nate's* woman makes it okay.

Nate and his merry band of men leave the apartment getting ready to tie everything down to make sure it's safe for the drive to Pelican Bay. I take a moment to glance around the empty apartment. I'm happy to leave and start my new adventure with Nate, but still a little sad to see this place go. Emma and I shared this home as we restarted our life. It's where I fell in love with Nate.

"Are you ready?" Tabitha asks.

I nod. This is it and I'm ready to start the next leg of my life. "I'm just not used to this whole group thing. Everyone is so nice." And none of the men let any of us women pick up anything. It was weird and a little awesome. I mean, I support feminism and all — making my way and handling my own boxes — but in truth it was nice not having to lift anything heavy. Very different from when I moved into the apartment.

"Trust me, Josie, you are about to get a lot of practice because you're one of us now."

"One of us who?"

"Well, whatever we are, don't call us the Bakery Bandits around Katy." Tabitha laughs while covering her mouth.

Katy scowls, pushing her on the shoulder. "That is not cool. When I figure out who gave us a name, they are in big trouble."

I don't think Katy's ever going to figure it out. Nobody will admit it. Not with knowing they face Katy's wrath.

"Are you girls ready to go?" Nate asks, leaning his head back into the apartment. "The trucks are loaded and we want to roll out."

Tabitha and Katy walk out as Nate holds the door, but I stay behind giving the apartment one last look.

Nate leans down, whispering in my ear. "I promise it will be a lot better where we're going."

He's right. I glance up, looking into his beautiful eyes with a smile. "I know."

THE REST of the weekend passes in a blur and before I realize it, I'm back in the thick of things with my previous life. Well, previous life, but at our new home in Pelican Bay rather than the apartment I made so many memories in with Emma.

"I don't have time to drive into Pelican Bay now, Josie,"

my ex says, sounding perpetually pissed off. "If you're moving into the city, you have to deal with the consequences."

I roll my eyes thankful he can't see. Here we go again. Another lecture from Barry about consequences. I guess because I didn't want to jump right back into bed and perform my *marital duties* after having a baby, his affair was also one of my consequences.

"It's not my fault you left your house late, Barry." It always amazes me how after years of marriage and our divorce, I still haven't learned that fighting with him doesn't help. He just pisses me off so much. I didn't allow myself to get pissed with him while we were married because I wanted to pretend it was all fine. But life with Barry was not fine and now when I'm able to get ticked, I can't shut the emotions off even when I should.

"It is your fault I had to drop her off. You were supposed to pick Emma up this time." Even though I can't see his face, I can picture the look he's giving me. Barry always had a way with snotty faces. "Don't ask me to do any favors for you in the future if this is the way you plan to act after getting your way."

"Noted," I say through gritted teeth. I never planned on asking for another favor anyway. "Look, Barry, I have to let you go so I can drive. Stoplights and all that," I say, disconnecting from his call at the turn onto the main road out of Pelican Bay — the one covered in trees and wooded acres and not a traffic light or stop sign in sight.

I turn the music up loud so I can legitimately say I didn't hear if he calls back.

The weekend with Nate was wonderful. We spent time unboxing all our possessions and mashing two households together, and in the evenings, we threw a big barbecue in our new backyard with our friends. It was the first of many perfect weekends. I can't wait to bring Emma home and have her look at her new place. She'll love her big room and the fenced-in backyard.

I pull into the apartment parking lot in my favorite space, deciding to use my key one last time. I need to turn it into the leasing office tomorrow, but I can use it tonight to relive a few memories of our time in this apartment. It is, after all, a place that led to so many other good things. I'm one of those women who likes to live the sappy all over again anytime possible. It's important to hold on to the good memories and special times while we can. It's also why I watch the Hallmark Channel Christmas movies over and over again during the month of December. We all know how they will end, but we watch anyway because the ending doesn't matter, only the journey. Nate better brace for many holidays spent with mugs of hot cocoa watching small-town romances on the big screen.

I step onto the sidewalk as a car pulls up to the space I just vacated. The driver rolls his window down.

"Hey!" he hollers.

Two men are in the front seat, but the one in the back seat puts me on high alert from the start. Anyone with three men in a vehicle would make me a little jittery, but I do my best to remember we're safe here.

"Can I help you?" I ask as I move closer to the car believing he wants directions.

"Yeah, you the hoe who stole our merchandise?"

I look around, and my body freezes at the mention of drugs. Who are these men and how do they know me?

18

"Who me?" I ask, putting a hand on my chest like it's not possible they could mean me. But my wide eyes give me away. They dart around anywhere and everywhere except looking at the men in the car as I back up.

The one behind the wheel, an overweight white man with slicked-back hair and dark sunglasses I only thought California troopers wore, laughs. "Yeah, that's her. Grab her, boys."

Two car doors open and I turn, my eyes wide like a bunny stuck in a trap. I run in the first direction I can. Straight ahead. It's Sunday, and the office is closed, but if I can reach an apartment in the building, there's a chance someone will help me. I veer left, turning hard and heading toward the apartment building, but something finds my back like a heavy bag of potatoes and knocks me to the ground.

I open my mouth wide, preparing to scream, but he clamps a hand over my lips and pushes so hard I can't even bite down. The man on top of me smells like he dumped a bottle of cologne on himself to cover up the fact he bathes in an old ashtray, and I try to gag but the pressure from his hand stops even that.

"Here's what you do, sweetheart. We're going to walk to the car together nice and slow. You scream and my friend will shoot you. It's that simple. Do you understand?"

I nod because what else can I do in that situation? I suck in a deep breath but don't get much oxygen because his hand blocks my mouth and nose as he pulls me up to standing. The two of us march back to the car with the other man following close behind, his angry eyes never leaving my focus.

"Why do they always run?" The guy in the front seat asks out his window.

I'm thrown into the middle of the backseat, each man flinging an arm over my chest to make sure I can't get out of the car and roll away. Which was my first and only thought at the moment. It's a tight fit and all three of us are breathing deeply as the driver puts the car in drive and pulls out.

"Who are you? What are you going to do?" I ask, gasping for breath from my unsuccessful attempt at escape.

Nobody answers.

"Where are you taking me?"

The driver's eyes meet mine in the rearview mirror and he sneers. "Listen up, lady. I'm the one who asks the questions, not you. Shut her up back there."

A hand slaps my face and the skin under my cheek burns as I rub away his red finger marks using the mirror to look at my swollen skin. My hair is a wild mess and my lip hurts as if a tooth cut it when I fell down.

Is this a kidnapping? I've never been kidnapped before? I'm not sure what you're supposed to do. Call the police or not call the police? Not that they would let me call 911, anyway.

I mentally kick myself, too scared to move in the car unless they find another way to shut me up. This time permanently. Why didn't I listen to Nate when he told me he wanted to come with me? I was so worried about getting Emma on time that I told him I couldn't wait for him to get back from the office. It would've been maybe an extra five minutes, but it would have meant a very different ending to the situation. All the things people say about small towns being safe are crap. They didn't poll this town.

What will happen to Emma if they kill me? She'd be forced to live with her father and the horrible babysitter as the only people to take care of her. I can't allow that to happen. As we drive further out of town headed into Clearwater, the two years of her life pass before me. The time she cut her first tooth and kept me up all night crying. When she took her first steps and then fell against the couch and bumped her head on the leg. Trick-or-treating and her first birthday party with all her family and friends. We're only a few months away from a birthday — one I couldn't wait to spend with her and Nate.

The events I've lived flash before my eyes but also all the stuff I'm missing out on in the future. A life with Nate. The children we would have, with his beautiful eyes and maybe my smile. Definitely his hair, the thick dark strands, which look like they take a ton of time to fix just right, but in reality he only runs his fingers through and goes. Would we have another daughter or son? We've talked hypothetical children here and there, but nothing concrete. Does he want one or two or five? I believe I'm particular to three myself, but if I wanted to live in the little yellow house for a lifetime, we'd better stop at two. There are all the barbecues we haven't had together. Our friends hanging out at our place on weekends. Homecoming games and prom dances for Emma and her siblings. Teaching her to drive. It's not the past, but all the things I'll miss out on hurt the most.

Calm down, Josie. Everything will be fine.

Everything is will be okay.

What the fuck am I thinking? Of course, it is not going to be okay. I'm in a car with three guys looking for their stolen drugs. I'm in deep shit.

A phone rings, the tune a Beatles song, and everyone in the car looks to me.

"Oh." It's mine.

Without thinking, I reach into my back pocket and pull out the cell phone I stashed there when I stepped out of the car at the apartment building.

"Hello, Nate?" I say, not sure it's him even though his named blinked on the screen.

"Josie, where are you? Is everything okay?" He sounds frantic and rushed. "Winnie is at the apartment with Emma and says your car is there but you aren't."

"I've been kidnapped!" I yell into the phone as the man to my right tugs it out of my grip. "Nate!"

"Shut up, lady." The tall guy who tackled me pulls his hand back like he's ready to slap me again. He takes the phone from his partner. "Is this Nate? The Pelican Bay Security Nate?" He's smiling and his head bobs back and forth like he's having fun during the madness happening around us. Obviously he's a true psycho.

There's a beat of silence as Nate yells on the other end.

"Is that so? I'd like to see you cut off my dick with finger nail clippers. I bet we could make some money at the side show," he says and laughs.

There's more yelling from Nate and the man's face falls at whatever he hears. "I'd advise you to not follow us. We're just going to ask your friend some questions, get back our stolen product, and then we'll return her. Probably safe and sound. It depends how forthcoming she is," he says leering in my direction and wearing a smile, which freezes my blood.

The power window is lowered and the guy tosses my cell phone out on the road without a second of warning.

"Hey!" I turn, watching the phone bounce once on the asphalt and then fall into the ditch. "I just bought that."

"If you live through this, I'm sure your boyfriend will buy you a new one," the guy driving the car says.

I swallow and turn back around to face the front.

The car slows and we turn, pulling into the parking lot of what has to be an abandoned building on the outskirts of Clearwater. The sides are covered in rusting metal and the roof has a hole in the top with so many tiles missing I bet you can see clear through the top.

"Get out of the car," the one sitting next to me says after he gets out first and leans back in the open doorway.

I stand my ground. Well, sit my ground since I'm in the back of the car. "No thanks. I don't want to."

"Get out," he says more forcefully this time.

"But the car is so nice. Why don't we stay here?" I pat the seat beside me. In reality it's horrible. There's a crack in the fake leather seats and is smells like somebody dropped a bag of Cheetos mixed with nachos sauce and let it marinate in the sun. For a year.

The area surrounding the warehouse is covered in trees and I've watched enough monster movies to know I don't want to go down any dark trails with somebody who has no problems with bumping me off. And even if they don't take me down out in the woods and finish me old yeller style, the building looks as if it's about to fall over.

I'll be rubble fodder if a gust of wind hits it just right.

"Get out of the car before I shoot you," the driver says, pulling a gun out from underneath the front seat.

19

I put my hands up, because that's what you do when someone is pointing a gun at you, and slide my butt off the seat. "Okay, okay."

"You don't want to be late for your meeting."

I shuffle toward the front of the warehouse, grateful they haven't walked me into the woods. You know your life has gone to shit when you're grateful to be going into a falling down building and not taking a shot to the back. "Late for my meeting?"

"The boss," the tallest guy of the three says. "Make sure and be respectful."

I hold my eye roll. I'm sure the seedy underbelly of Pelican Bay needs respect.

The door to the warehouse is shoved open but once I walk through, it's propped close again. The empty building has a thick layer of dust covering the ground and also floating in the air. I cough, twice, my allergies already annoyed as fuck I'm here. They aren't the only parts.

"Take a seat," the driver says, pointing to a lone chair sitting in the middle of the warehouse.

That's weird, but what's weirder is the old-style television set someone placed on one of those rolling carts they used in schools twenty years ago. It's just like six grade health class when they made us watch all the sex ed videos with the lights on.

"Your boss is a TV?" I ask because now I'm thoroughly confused.

"Shut up and sit down," he says.

I hold back the smartass retort about not moving.

Once my butt is in the chair and I've laid my hands in my lap, my body goes tight waiting for a gun to be placed against the back of my head to take me out execution style. Instead the TV turns on and the staticky screen is filled with an image.

It's not one I expect. The camera pulls back like they're filming the guy for an address from the president's oval office. The man on the screen is no president. He's skinny with slicked-back hair and a face that would almost be cute if I wasn't stuck in a warehouse and he was apparently the boss. He's behind a large mahogany desk, which makes me think he's overcompensating for something as he sits drumming his fingers on the table. There's nothing presidential about him.

"There you are, Miss Summerton."

"Hi," I whisper. "Can he hear me?"

The guy in the television screen rolls his eyes. "Yes, I can hear you, dear."

I nod but then I'm not sure if he can see me either so I say, "Okay."

"My name is Antonio and I run a few operations on

the west side of the country. It's come to my attention that you and your friends stumbled upon a shipment of merchandise, which wasn't intended for you. Rather than leave and go about your day like a reasonable person, you entered the storage unit, looked through my boxes, and then put them in your car and drove away."

"How do you know that?"

He drums his fingers a few more times, not happy I'm asking questions, so I decide to shut up from here on out. "Every good storage facility has cameras, my dear."

"So far she hasn't talked, boss." The big guy who was driving the car steps forward while talking. He's obviously the leader of this dastardly trio.

The guy behind the desk rolls his eyes. "I assumed so since no one called and told me where the drugs were, you moron! That's why we have Josie here to answer questions."

"I don't know where they are," I say truthfully.

"That's a problem. Because, you see, I need them. With certain acquaintances out of the business," he says the words way too happily, making me think he had something to do with them getting *out of the business*. "I've had to expand operations rather quickly, and your friend Ridge has hired someone to spy on me. Now I don't think they picked up any useful information, but it's a weird coincidence my men tracked them right back to Pelican Bay where a few women stole so many pounds of products. Isn't that odd?" he asks.

I nod. "It is, but I swear it was just an accident. I don't know what happened."

"You understand why it's hard for me to believe you?" he says, almost sincerely.

And the problem is I see how it could be a problem. Were Hannah and Lukis spying on him? Is that why they booked it to Pelican Bay as Hannah said?

"I don't want to die, so I promise if I knew I would tell you." Drugs aren't worth my life.

"Where did you take it after you drove away?"

I swallow and hesitate. I may not know where the drugs are now, but I remember where we took them. I won't lead them to Anessa's bakery.

"Listen, I'm 99 percent sure they're not still there."

"But why don't you tell me where you went and let us figure out where they are."

I shake my head. "No." I won't do it to Anessa.

"You seem to be confused. I have intel that says Lukis and his whore, Hannah, were in Pelican Bay. They talked to Ridge Jefferson. The problem is I don't know how you found the drugs before my guys got there. Did they call ahead and have a drop point?"

"No," I say truthfully, my brain trying to work around all his accusations. Lukis and Hannah knew there were drugs in the storage unit?

"I want to find my drugs!" he yells, his fist slamming on the table with the resounding bang echoing. "Tell me!"

With his raised voice, I jump at least an inch off my chair. "I don't know," I say choking back tears. Something tells me the crying won't help me out here.

Antonio shakes his head and then nods once at the man standing behind me. "Make her talk," he says.

There's a screeching sound on the floor and I turn in time to catch them slide a rectangular table a few feet until it's next to my chair.

Antonio smiles on the video screen and it means not good things for me.

"Give me your hand," the chubby man says.

I clench both hands to my chest, sticking my fingers underneath my arms. "No." Do they think I'm a moron? No one's touching my hands. I like them and my fingers. I'm attached.

"Boys, why don't you help our friend out," Antonio says, and I slap myself for thinking he could almost be cute if he wasn't a mob boss. The man has psychological problems.

The two men who rode in the car's backseat with me each tug an arm until I'm unable to keep it tucked away. "I swear I don't. I promise!" It doesn't stop them.

Together they take my hand and pry my fingers apart until they're set flat on the small table beside me. Bile curls in my stomach and threatens to come up as I gag with imagery of what they're about to do. I like my fingers. All of them.

"Which one do you want, boss," the driver asks.

My eyes search them out, begging and pleading for him to make a different choice. "I swear I don't know."

I gag again and Antonio smiles. "Start with the little one."

"No!" I work to tuck my fingers back into a fist but he applies more pressure, leaning his entire body weight on my hand and cracking the knuckles.

20

Glass shatters and I fling my body forward out of instinct more than anything else. They pull my arm back as a large body soars through the air. It's the limp form of one of the guys. In the commotion I pull my hand away and tuck it into myself, rolling into a small ball on the floor.

A thick head of hair — one that's easy to make out as Nate — tackles the driver to the floor, his fist punching him in the head.

"Get Josie!" he yells. Our eyes lock in for a second and the world stops as I stare at him, hopeful he's come to rescue me. The first sign of a tear trickles down my face as the commotion picks back up again in rapid speed. *Now is not the time to cry, stupid.* Why do my tears always come at the worst times?

Two hands grab me and I hit my attacker as hard as possible, doing everything I can to wiggle away as he picks me up in his arms and clutches me close to his chest.

"Shhh, Josie. I've got you, it's me." I struggle, but look up and see a pair of eyes belonging to a man I've met before.

My heart clutches in my chest. "Crispin?" It's not Nate but another one of Ridge's team.

He squeezes me tighter and carries me away from the melee happening on the floor in the warehouse. "I've got you. You're okay."

I shake my head no. "I don't feel okay." Where's Nate? Why isn't he following us out?

"Are you hurt anywhere? Bleeding? Did anyone touch you?"

"No." My injuries aren't physical. Crispin carries me outside, and the sun hits my face, stinging my eyes and forcing me to clench them closed.

There's yelling as more men from Ridge's barbecue race into the warehouse. Panic and mayhem ensue everywhere.

"Put her down and step away," a harsh voice utters.

Crispin laughs and puts me down on the ground, keeping me steady until my feet touch. "She's all yours," he says.

I turn and Nate stands three feet away. "Josie."

I don't wait for whatever else comes next. I run into his arms and throw myself into them, hopeful Nate can catch me.

He does. Our lips come together, and he wraps me up in his warmth, his arms circling my body, but his heart securing my soul.

"You saved me." I hug him harder, the tears flowing down my face.

"I will always save you," he says.

Ridge's men lead three of the attackers out of the warehouse, each of their hands tied behind their backs with white zip ties. I glare at each one. From here on out, Nate will never need to do anything to save me again. I'll live a nice quiet life where I never leave our little yellow house. Definitely no more hanging out with Katy.

NATE PULLS a few strands of my hair back, tucking them behind my shoulder, and runs a thumb against the skin behind my ear. It started out cute. I thought he was caressing me in a loving way, but the way his head moves closer to one area as if he's studying me it's easy to figure out this is something different.

I bat his hand away. "Nate, it's been twenty-four hours. I'm fine." The man has hovered around me since my rescue yesterday. At first I thought it was wonderful. I loved having his attention. Now I kinda want to go back to work. He's even checking over Emma and she wasn't even there.

"I thought I saw a bruise forming."

"The only thing bruised," I say, bashing my phone as hard as possible against the granite countertops in my new kitchen, "is my phone."

I hit it on the counter two more times before Nate carefully grabs it from my hands.

"They said this case was indestructible, but there's something wrong with it."

Nate inspects the case and the top of the phone for any cracks, but I told him the case is supposed to be indestructible. "It did get flung onto the road from a moving car," he says still studying the spotless phone.

"Indestructible case." It's the only way I dare own a smart phone, which cost as much as an expensive laptop when you're a parent.

He slips the phone in his back pocket. "I told you your carrier sucks. It won't work in this part of Pelican Bay. I'll get you a new one."

"Everyone always says phones don't work in Pelican Bay, but that is crazy. It doesn't make sense. It worked before how can a cell not work here now?" Sure, I had a bad signal in the bakery, but I thought it was the brick building.

"They work. You just need the right carrier." He shrugs, leaning across the counter and getting close again. "Forget the phone. I'll fix the phone. Are you okay?" he asks, staring into my eyes.

"Yes." I remind myself not to get frustrated because at one point in time I had a husband who didn't care if I was okay. I can't be looking a gift horse in the mouth. If Nate wants to fawn all over me, then so be it. I'll be fawned over. It's not a hardship.

He leans over the counter ticking one finger from his hand out. "I promise you we are going to hunt Antonio down and stop his organization. They won't set foot within one hundred miles of Pelican Bay when I'm done with them."

A shiver runs through my body and I flex my fingers before bringing them into a fist. My pinky throbs.

Why did he have to be named Antonio? I can never eat my favorite pizza place back in Bangor again.

"So, what's on the agenda this week?" I ask Nate, trying to bring some normality back to our lives.

He thinks for a moment, tapping his finger on the counter. "Number one, absolutely no drama."

I nod, on board with this plan. No more drama, ever.

"Number two, I want you and Emma to stay here and enjoy the new house while you can."

I smile. "What are you going to do?"

Nate grabs my hand, pulling me close, and places a kiss on my lips. "I'll go to work every day to make this town safe and spend every night making you scream my name in pleasure."

Yes, this will be a very good life indeed.

EPILOGUE
NATE

A few weeks later

Sunlight shines through the thin curtains Josie picked out to go in our master bedroom. They're a light color she calls rose and I call pink. I'm not sure what happened to my fucking manhood that I'm allowing pink curtains in my bedroom, but I plan to run with it for the time being.

Although something has to be done about keeping the light out. Hell, I'd buy pink blackout curtains if they would make her happy. We could get some blinds up in here. Anything to stop the weekend morning sun from waking me up.

Josie twitches in her sleep and I wrap my arm around her, pulling her back to my chest. She sinks into my arms and relaxes, falling back to sleep.

This is what I work so hard for. I stick my face in the

back of her hair, breathing deeply with the smell of strawberries tickling my senses. It's wonderful. I've never been so happy and I know the people around me are happy for me.

The rest of my life will be spent with Josie and Emma. Every day I'll work to do a better job keeping them protected while adding a few more kids of our own. First, we need to get married and then we can have little Josies running around before we add a few boys to the mix.

My phone buzzes on the nightstand and I reach over, grabbing it so it doesn't wake up Josie. It's a text from Crispin.

CRISPIN: Pizza tonight Roadhouse Bar. Don't be late.

NATE: I'm skipping this one. Next time.

CRISPIN: Really dude? Why?

NATE: One day you'll find her and will skip out too. More important things, man.

He texts back immediately.

CRISPIN: That woman does not exist.

He is wrong. She exists, he just hasn't found her... yet.

I can only hope he doesn't hit her with his truck. I laugh, jiggling the bed, and Josie rolls over to put her face in my chest.

Emma whines in her crib, yelling out for her mom, and Josie sighs. She knows she has to get up, but she doesn't want to. I kiss her on the forehead in my favorite spot with a tiny little freckle that sticks out from her hairline. "I got her. Go back to sleep."

Her head sinks into the pillow and I give it another second, watching her fall back into a peaceful sleep before I slowly crawl out of bed and make my way to Emma's room.

I hope the rest of my life with Josie and Emma is calm with no more interruptions, but something tells me when you live in Pelican Bay and hang around with the people we do, there's only going to be a lot more fun to come.

Before I met Josie, I lived a nice calm and ordered life. Everything had its place, but then she walked into my world with Emma on her hip and nothing has been the same since. I love every crazy minute of it. I couldn't ask for anything more from the woman I want to spend the rest of my life with from here until eternity.

Before I can calm down, settle into our new home life, and start a future with Josie, I need to make sure we eliminate all threats. We can't allow Antonio Gambo to continue his operation in the area. Now more than ever it's time to bring down the men who threaten Pelican Bay.

Looking for the next book in The Pelican Bay Security series? You can now buy Accidental Risk on all retailers. To stay up to date on new releases and receive two free books sign up for my newsletter.

Keep reading for an excerpt from Accidental Risk

THANK YOU!

Thank you for reading Lifetime Risk! If you'd like to find out more about the stories in Pelican Bay or read my other series you can find information about all of my books on my website:

http://www.authormeganmatthews.com

You can also visit the town of Pelican Bay online at:

http://pelicanbaymaine.com/

Fans can also join my Facebook Reader Group for the inside track on what's happening behind the scenes, special giveaways, and advanced reader copies of new books.

ACCIDENTAL RISK SNEAK PEEK

Continue reading for a sneak peek of Accidental Risk

ACCIDENTAL RISK PROLOGUE
CRISPIN

E very once in a while, you come across a special moment in life when something happens and you recognize your future has shifted permanently. You'll wake up the next morning, and nothing will ever be the same again.

This wasn't one of those moments.

"Here, Crispin, I opened it for you," Elliot says as he passes me the light-colored beer bottle and I take my first sip of the refreshing brew. We'd both fallen in love with the cheap imported beer, Sol, after a three-month-long mission on the streets of Mexico. It was our first mission for Ridge Jefferson before we officially joined his special forces team based in Pelican Bay, Maine.

He laughed when I packed a six-pack in my carry-on bag but lamented the day I drank the last one. It wasn't until four months later while shopping in a crappy little store in Clearwater that I found one of their coolers packed with the stuff. The guys and I always joked the maker couldn't sell it in America because they used water with a case of Montezuma's revenge, a stomach illness tourists often contracted while visiting the area. Since then I've traveled once a month to the little store so my fridge always has a steady supply.

It's also made me the local hangout for the men in my new unit. We may no longer be Navy SEALs, but the four men Ridge assigned to our task force bonded as closely as when we were stuck in the desert with nothing to talk about except tits and ammo.

"I'm about to start this game even if you're not paying attention," he says, making me look away from the window. I wasn't only the hangout for my drink selection, I also had the big seventy-inch television and every single video game system known to man.

A man needed hobbies. In truth, killing zombies while taking over a mythical world full of dragons didn't hold as much excitement for me as the monstrosity taking place outside the enormous picture window in my living room.

"Dude, you are acting like a stalker."

I shrug but then question his words. Do I seem like a stalker? Can she see me? "You should see how bad she is at this, Elliot."

"Wouldn't it be crazier to find a woman good at it?"

I shake my head because Elliot didn't understand the true depth of the situation. "She ran over his Azalea bushes." The pink flowers had become over grown during the spring and into the summer, but now they look like Edward Scissorhands had a drunken visit in the night.

"I find it more concerning that you know the flower name."

I roll my eyes and follow his character into the cave, keeping one eye out the window. "My grandmother was a master gardener. She used to pay me five bucks a flower bed when I visited every summer." When you're a poor kid from New York, five bucks times fifteen beds is a hell of a lot of money.

"The dude won't even notice when he gets home."

"Are you kidding me? My neighbor is like a 1950s suburban husband. His grass is his child." I'm surprised I've never caught him out there with a ruler making sure it was all cut the same length. The man loved his yard. He mowed it, fertilized, and even put down new mulch in the spring and the fall, which I considered a little overkill, but the guy had a green thumb. He would flip when he returned home and saw his new woman had mowed down half his bushes and ruined the crisscrossing zigzag lines he created when he mowed. Instead she'd replaced them with the mismatched figure eight routine she made up on her own as if she was dancing to whatever music played in her headphones. The place had gone from heaven to horticultural murder scene.

"Kill that skeleton for me," Elliot yells louder than necessary and my character takes off in a dash chasing down the random skeleton that tried to escape the blockade we'd set up in the game.

My neighbor, Dalton, had a new woman in his place at least every week. I'd never seen the same girl twice, and he remembered none of their names. The current one had camped out three weeks, and she started mowing the lawn two weeks ago. Today she'd put the final piece of her destruction on the flower beds she'd forgotten existed earlier in the month.

She had to be somebody special if he kept her around this long. Although, from the look of his front yard, she wouldn't make it much longer. Once he saw her hack job, she'd be on a bus out of town.

"Have you seen Dalton? Maybe he's okay with the yard."

"No, I haven't in at least four weeks. He's probably out on a mission." It would be fireworks when he returned home. No one wanted to come back combat weary and look at the blood bath waiting for him at his place of comfort.

"It's possible she killed him, buried him in the basement, and she's taken over his house."

We walk deeper into the caves together and I select a lantern from my inventory to help light the way. "Really, you think?"

"No, dumbass, but you've turned into a Mrs. Kravitz. Back away from the window before it gets even creepier. You'll have Detective Anderson at your door and then Ridge will follow him to kick your ass for putting the police on our radar."

We reached the end of the cave and wielded our pick-axes to bust through the wall, looking for a secret entrance. "It will be a blowup."

Elliot laughs. "You can let her cry on your shoulder and then show her a real man doesn't give a fuck about the flowers once he kicks her to the curb." He glances in my direction and smirks, giving me warning he has more to say and I wouldn't like it. "Oh, but wait, you do. Send her my way and I'll make sure she's properly sympathized."

I roll my eyes and use my character to hit him in the

game, taking a heart away from his overall health before I toss him a bottle of instant healing.

The problem is he spoke the truth. I didn't mind if the mysterious woman showed up at my door looking for a shoulder to cry on once he got rid of her. I wasn't one for sloppy seconds, but she was gorgeous. Dark brown hair fell past her shoulders, and her ass filled out a pair of Daisy Dukes. I would let her trim my bushes any day of the week.

AVAILABLE NOW AT YOUR FAVORITE ONLINE
RETAILER

MORE BOOKS BY MEGAN MATTHEWS

THE BOYS OF RDA SERIES

Rush

Lag

Glitch - fan exclusive

Grind

Beta

Quest

Hack

PELICAN BAY SECURITY SERIES

Security Risk

Future Risk

Holiday Risk

Sweetest Risk

Quickest Risk

Aloha Cowboy

Biggest Risk
Lifetime Risk
Accidental Risk
Family Risk

ABOUT THE AUTHOR

Megan Matthews writes smutty romance by day and hides behind her secret identity as a responsible Pinterest mom when other parents are around. She believes morning shouldn't start until noon and chocolate should be calorie free. Living in Michigan she prefers sun over snow, hot chocolate over coffee, and wine over beer.

Preferring books over nature, Megan once displayed the entire Goosebumps series on her bookshelf. Her taste in reading has matured. She now prefers her heroes with rippling muscles naked in bed over brace-faced nerds running from murderous dummies.

You can follow her online at all the usual places.

Printed in Great Britain
by Amazon

24260234R10136